He looked up at h... around her waist and pulled... him, kissing her deeply until it felt as if her breath left her and became his.

"We're going to get married."

She couldn't have been more shocked if the ground had opened up beneath her feet. "We are?"

"Yes. As soon as possible. Tomorrow."

Rose moved away from his side, trying to take in what was the strangest proposal she'd ever heard. "Why are we doing this?"

"Because I need to take care of you."

She blinked. "I'm taking care of myself just fine. But thank you for the offer. I guess."

He shook his head. "It's not an offer. It's a marriage proposal. I want you to marry me."

"I always heard Callahans were terribly hard to tie down. That they avoid the altar like the plague." She moved to the opposite side of the table. "What's going through your head, Callahan?"

Dear Reader,

In this thirteenth book of the Callahan Cowboys miniseries, Galen Callahan is long overdue a love of his own. His eye has been caught by Rose Carstairs, who proves herself worthy of the lifestyle of the New Mexico clan. Rose has always wanted the hunky Callahan for her own—but finding herself pregnant with triplets isn't the way she wanted to catch him!

I hope you'll join me for this latest story in the Callahan saga as family loyalties are explored and true love is tested. The family bond is as strong as the land—and Rose and Galen will need every bit of that strength to find their way to each other at long last.

Best wishes and happy endings always,

Tina Leonard

www.tinaleonard.com
www.facebook.com/tinaleonardbooks
www.facebook.com/authortinaleonard
www.twitter.com/Tina_Leonard

A CALLAHAN
CHRISTMAS MIRACLE

—

TINA LEONARD

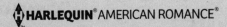
HARLEQUIN® AMERICAN ROMANCE®

Recycling programs
for this product may
not exist in your area.

ISBN-13: 978-0-373-75477-9

A CALLAHAN CHRISTMAS MIRACLE

Copyright © 2013 by Tina Leonard

Printed in U.S.A.

HARLEQUIN®
www.Harlequin.com

ABOUT THE AUTHOR

Tina Leonard is a *USA TODAY* bestselling and award-winning author of more than fifty projects, including several popular miniseries for the Harlequin American Romance line. Known for bad-boy heroes and smart, adventurous heroines, her books have made the *USA TODAY*, Waldenbooks, Ingram and Nielsen BookScan bestseller lists. Born on a military base, Tina lived in many states before eventually marrying the boy who did her crayon printing for her in the first grade. You can visit her at www.tinaleonard.com, and follow her on Facebook and Twitter.

Books by Tina Leonard

HARLEQUIN AMERICAN ROMANCE

Much gratitude to all the loyal and supportive readers who have taken the Callahans into their hearts—this book is for you.

"Those Callahans come from fine stock. We've had our differences, but you end up respecting everything they stand for."

—Bode Jenkins to a reporter, when asked why he'd given up the feud between their neighboring ranches

Chapter One

Galen Chacon Callahan looked over Rancho Diablo, where dark smoke filled the sky above the canyons with smudges of black. He put his binoculars to his eyes, studying the smoke as it grew and thickened.

He turned as his sister, Ashlyn, drove up in the jeep. "It's not a wildfire," she said.

"No." Rancho Diablo was safely separated from the fire by the canyons, but if someone was sending up signals near the expansive ranch, it would be a message the Callahans couldn't ignore. "It's the land Storm Cash has offered to sell us."

"I know. I wonder if the elderly farmer who sold that land to Storm still lives there." She studied Galen's face. "Think we should ride over and check on him?"

"I'll call the sheriff. He can alert the proper authorities. I think it's best if we stay out of it for now." He was troubled by the fire, and an uneasy feeling was growing in the pit of his stomach. "I'm heading back."

"I'll stay here a bit longer."

"Got your gun?" Galen asked, knowing full well that Ash could take care of herself. He could order her back to the ranch—*should* order her—but she'd just ignore him. Probably give him a blistering retort to send him on his way, as well.

"When do I not have my gun?" Ash didn't even bother to glance at him. Her eyes were glued to the horizon.

"Don't go over there."

"I won't. Quit fussing. You're like a mother hen." Ash finally turned to look him in the eye. "By the way, the new agents are at the house, waiting for you to interview them."

"New agents?"

"The ones to replace Ana and River. Jace lined them up every hour on the hour for interviews. Remember we agreed we needed new agents? Sawyer Cash can't handle everything on her own. And anyway," Ash muttered under her breath, though he could plainly hear every word of her complaint, "I'm not exactly sure she's capable of handling anything."

He'd listened to all the negative things the Callahan clan said about Sawyer, and he couldn't say there wasn't real reason for concern. She was Storm Cash's niece, after all, and they'd never been certain if they could trust their wily neighbor. He always seemed to be in the wrong place at the right time. "Maybe we're just being suspicious," Galen said.

"There's no such thing as too much caution."

"I know. I'm heading off. Be careful. Don't invite trouble." Even though he knew Ash was more than capable of protecting not just herself but the ranch, Galen couldn't help leaving his sister with that warning before riding toward Rancho Diablo's main house. After last month, when their aunt Fiona blew up Uncle Wolf's hideout in Montana, he and his brothers had decided that the women in their family had earned their stripes. They could more than take care of themselves. Ash, like the rest of them, had been in the military, a trained operative. She was as tough as any male Callahan. Tougher, maybe. And so he and his five brothers had finally decided that their overprotective attitude toward their baby sister was accomplishing nothing and was detrimental to their family harmony.

Ash had never listened to anyone's concerns, anyway. Like Fiona, and the women who'd married into the Callahan family, she did what she wanted—which was mostly chase Xav Phillips, a family employee who rode the canyons and kept an eye out for trespassers.

Galen was pretty sure Ash caught him on occasion, too.

He was so busy pondering the smoke in the canyons and his platinum-haired baby sister that he almost missed the rider heading his way. A brunette he didn't recognize rode up on a gray horse.

"Hi," she said, smiling, as if it was every day strange women appeared at Rancho Diablo.

"Hello?" He swallowed, peering into the dark green eyes smiling at him from under a white cowgirl hat.

Her smile turned sweeter, somehow sexy. Galen tried to pull his brain back from the alluring abyss into which it was threatening to fall. "My name's Somer Stevens. I'm here to apply for the agent position."

"I believe the agents are supposed to be waiting for their interviews up at the house."

"There are ten candidates over there right now. It's not every day that an opening comes up for a position at Rancho Diablo." Somer winked conspiratorially. "I figured I'd better take a look around before I decided whether I belong here or not."

He frowned. "My brothers were going to show everyone around."

"Yes, but if I'd waited for the canned tour, I wouldn't have gotten to speak to you directly."

Direct. Assertive. These were valuable traits in someone working for the Callahans. Most likely he would've done the same thing, if he'd been in her shoes. But he wasn't, and he was going to let her know that stroking his ego wasn't going to get her anywhere.

This one wasn't getting the job. Somer didn't follow directions, and she made him sweat. She wore dark blue pants and a blue jacket, all very proper for an interview. She had a great horse and a lot of attitude, yet something told him Somer was nothing but trouble.

And he never ignored his instincts.

UNUSUAL MOMENT NUMBER TWO of Galen's day was when he walked into the massive den at Rancho Diablo, looking for Fiona and the others. He wanted to corral his brothers into the upstairs library, where they always held their meetings, so he could set a game plan before they began interviewing. Galen wanted to apprise his brothers of Somer's tactic, and make certain she didn't win her way into the job by pulling the same thing on them that she had on him.

He gawked at the woman sitting demurely in the den, recognizing her from one of Fiona's many Christmas balls in Diablo. She wore a gypsy costume and flashed a big smile he found irresistible. "I believe I know you."

"I'm Rose Carstairs." She shook his hand, and it was crazy how much he enjoyed feeling her small hand in his. "You were there the night Dante was raffled off. Will it be your turn this year?"

He found himself transfixed by her costume, which consisted of a flouncy black skirt that fell to her knees, a fluffy white blouse, lots of dangling chains around her neck and huge hoop earrings. She wore many thin bracelets, and her blond hair was swept up in a bouncy ponytail, topped by a red rose. "That's some outfit you're wearing."

"I'm here to apply for the bodyguard position."

Galen laughed. "You don't look the type."

"Isn't that the point?"

He watched her full lips curve into a smile. Appreciated the sparkle in her blue eyes. "I don't see how you'd blend into the background, gorgeous."

"Hello, Galen," Aunt Fiona said, bustling into the den. "Don't stand there monopolizing the talent, please. You have interviews waiting."

"The talent?" He looked at Rose.

"I see you've met Rose," Fiona said. "She's applying for the nanny position."

"Ah. The nanny position." Galen took a second look at her shapely calves, her flat black, practical shoes, and the laughter in Rose's eyes. "I should have known."

"Come on, dear," Fiona said, "before Galen hires you to be his *personal* bodyguard. Goodness, Galen, get a move on. You need to change, look like a respectable employer."

Rose grinned at him. "Good luck."

"Good luck to you. Nice to meet you, Rose." He went off, forcing himself not to watch her curvy backside as she followed Fiona out of the room. It was clear his aunt was interested in hiring her. He didn't think his brothers would get a thing done with Rose around. The scenery would be just too tempting.

Then it occurred to him that he and Jace were the only bachelors left at Rancho Diablo. Sawyer was doing her best to monopolize Jace, though Galen wasn't certain how effective her barrage of attention was on his brother's single status.

But that left him as the lone available Callahan. The Lone Ranger of Rancho Diablo.

Neither Rose nor Somer might make the cut with his five brothers and headstrong sister. His brothers were dumb as woolly mammoths, and his sister, well, Ash was unpredictable at best. Her mind stayed on Xav Phillips. She could go thumbs-up or thumbs-down on either woman. Plus, there were a number of other applicants.

He was thumbs-way-up-high on Rose.

He'd just let the situation develop and hope that Rose and her playful, kid-friendly gypsy costume were voted *yes* by the family council. There was something so sexy and darling about a woman who came dressed to play.

Jace followed Galen into the upstairs library for the meeting. "Did you see that that woman from the Christmas ball year before last showed up?"

"I did." Galen ignored his brother while he dug through some paperwork. "Let's lay out our battle plan. We need a new strategy, or have to improve on the old one. Something has to change."

"I might ask her out," Jace said. "You know, she's from Tempest. Not that far down the road—and we've got family and friends there. Our cousins have the Dark Diablo ranch in Tempest. It's a nice place. And Rose is probably a real nice gal. Looks like it, anyway." He grinned at his brother.

Galen hesitated, suddenly losing interest in the stack of papers. "Why?"

"She's hot as an oven, dude."

Galen swallowed. "Poetic."

"I know, right?" Jace grinned, pleased with his announcement. "If Fiona hires her, I'm definitely going to think about it."

"I almost hate to ask, and we do have greater matters to discuss other than your love life, but don't you and Sawyer have kind of a secret thing going on?"

Jace shrugged. "If it's a secret, why are you asking? And no, we don't. Sawyer is a pretty girl. That's all. I think she flirts with all the guys. She'd probably flirt with you, if you'd unbend."

Galen decided he didn't care about Jace's love life. "Whatever."

"Why? Do you want to ask Rose out?"

"No, I don't." *Damn straight, I do.*

"Because if you want to," Jace said, like a dog with a juicy bone, "I wouldn't stand in the way. I wouldn't want to make you look bad. You're not getting any younger, old-timer."

"As if you could make me look bad." Galen glanced toward the door. "Where's the rest of the team?"

"I think they saw the other candidates and stopped to chat. I, on the other hand, stick to the assignment." Jace poured himself a whiskey with a huge grin. "What's up with your face, bro? Look like you have a stomachache. Need a soother?" He waved the bottle Galen's way.

"I do not need a soother." He sat on a sofa, dismissing his brother, and pondered what he should say about Somer. She'd definitely gone after the job, and he felt vaguely uneasy about her aggressiveness. He was the eldest Callahan, a doctor, a man who believed that fate and hard work brought many gifts. Why should Somer bother him so much?

"One of the candidates took off by herself to tour the ranch," Galen said.

"Oh." Jace seated himself at the opposite end of the sofa. "The tall, hot brunette? I think I heard Fiona tell her to go let her horse have some exercise. She pointed her in your direction, knowing the two of you would meet up. Fiona would never send a female onto the ranch without protection, but she knew you were on your way back, and that Ash was out there, too."

Now that made more sense. Aunt Fiona's fey mind at work, probably culling the tempting beauties from the herd and dangling them in front of the remaining single Callahans. "Why'd she bring her own horse?"

"Probably because she'd be expected to ride here? This is a ranch, you know."

It all sounded reasonable.

"Gorgeous piece of flesh, if you ask me." Jace's grin was so irritating Galen wished he could bean him one across the head as he had when they were children. He'd given up beaning his siblings when they went off to boot camp.

"Are you planning on asking her out or not?" Galen asked.

Jace gave him an annoyed look. "The *horse* was a gorgeous piece of horseflesh," he said, emphasizing the word as if Galen were stupid. Then he grinned again. "Galen, my brother, has a woman finally walked into your path that stirs your quiet, hard-to-reach soul?"

"No," he said, thinking, *Yes, that petite blonde with big eyes, but I'm not about to give you anything to crow about.*

The rest of their brothers filed in, as well as Ash, whose grin was big as the quarter moon.

"What's going on with the fire?" Galen asked her.

"Sheriff says he's got men over there checking it out. We'll know soon enough."

He studied his brothers, grateful that he'd been able to keep them on the right path, the path of men committed to the fight. Strong, brave, true. Of course, Grandfather Running Bear had set the path for all of them. When their parents had gone away from the tribe, Galen returned home from his medical studies and raised his brothers and sister. They'd been a headstrong bunch, fierce and courageous. All of them had opted to join the military—and then retired to quiet lives. Then Running Bear had reached out with his astonishing instructions that they come to Rancho Diablo and protect cousins they'd never known they had. Protect a heritage they'd never known was theirs.

That decision had been the turning point that marked them all, and changed their lives.

"Excuse me," Fiona said. Their aunt poked her head into the library. "I know the family meetings are sacred, but Rose is about to head back to Tempest. Are there any objections to her being hired on here?"

Jace looked at him. "Yes, Galen, are there any objections?"

Galen grimaced. "Why would I care who is hired as a nanny here? I don't have children."

"Well, you always seem to have an opinion about everything, relevant or not," Fiona replied. "And you've met Rose before, so I just wanted to make certain there'd be no awkwardness. Awkwardness is bad when we all live as closely as we do."

His frown deepened. "Why would I feel awkward around Rose? I barely know her."

The rest of the family was quick to sense that something was in the air.

"Are we roasting Galen about something, Aunt Fiona?" Ash asked.

"No. Just making sure his highness is consulted about the new hires." Fiona looked pleased with her jibe.

"Ah," Dante said, "you're trying not to get on his bad side by hiring Rose." He nodded wisely, as if he understood the entire situation. Galen felt pretty much in the dark. "So, Galen, what do you think about the new girl?"

Galen cleared his throat, realizing his family had him pinned against the wall. If he let on that he did have a weakness for Rose, there would be incessant teasing and subtle ribbing. "I couldn't care less who is hired on at Rancho Diablo." He pondered his words for a moment. "Though I do admit I'm not certain about Somer Stevens...."

Everyone said, "Ah!"

He sighed. "I guess I couldn't convince you that there's just something about her that puts me off. It's not personal." He glared around the room at all the smiling faces. "Never mind. I don't care who gets hired. Can we get on to planning how to beef up security?"

They moved on with the meeting, shooting him a few knowing looks, sizing up his mood in a way that family does when they know you've got something on your mind. His family did know him—very well—but on the matter of his heart, Galen preferred to remain an enigma.

Then he could romance Rose without his family observing every single move he made, the way they had with his brothers when they were courting. Of course,

Galen did the same thing to them, which was why he had no desire to have the matchmaking tongs applied to him. Once his family had you in their sights, the well-meaning interference never ended.

If Rose accepted the position, he'd begin to plan a different strategy, called Romancing the Nanny.

He didn't want to be the Lone Ranger of Rancho Diablo for the rest of his life.

"What are you grinning about, bro?" Tighe asked, and Galen shook himself from his daydream of Rose's delightful curves and big smile. "Look like you had something sweet on your mind."

"Just wondering how you dolts ever ended up with women. Proceed." He waved a hand imperiously. "Let's hear all your plans for securing this ranch, especially if that fire over there was set by our renegade uncle, Wolf. Because if it can happen across the canyons, it most certainly can happen at Rancho Diablo. And I refuse to allow the work of our father and Uncle Jeremiah to go up in smoke."

Chapter Two

Rose knew immediately she was going to like living at Rancho Diablo, and it wasn't just because of the long-term crush she'd had on Galen Callahan. He was just about the biggest hunk of delicious cowboy she'd ever seen. Tall, strong, with dark hair tumbling over his forehead and down the back of his neck—she got shivers just thinking about him.

She'd tried desperately to win him at the ball year before last, but Sawyer Cash had outbid everyone else. Rose figured Sawyer had needed a job really bad if she'd tried to grease the skids with winning bids.

Or maybe she'd just wanted a man. Rose thought about that. She could definitely see Sawyer Cash trying to catch a cowboy that way, by appealing to his ego.

Ego was something the Callahans didn't lack, for sure.

Fiona bustled into the kitchen. "You're hired!"

Rose smiled. "Thank you!"

"Now, when can you start?" Fiona pulled out a work-book and began inputting information.

"I can start as soon as you need me." Rose knew her father wouldn't be thrilled that she was taking this job—he said the Callahans were surrounded by danger and he didn't want his little girl around them—but she needed work, and this was perfect for what she liked to do best.

"That would be today," Fiona said. "We always need help, and we know you're hardworking and that we can trust you. I'll show you your room."

She followed Fiona up the stairs, amazed by the size and beauty of Rancho Diablo as they passed a large window. The working ranch was almost like a museum, but every building was styled by a decorator with an eye to classic comfort. "Your home is beautiful, Fiona."

"Your home, now, too." The older woman opened a door, revealing a spacious bedroom decorated in blue and white, with toile curtains. "If this suits you, this will be home sweet home. I picked this room because it's far enough from all the others that you can have some peace and quiet."

Rose wondered where Galen's room was. "This is perfect," she said. She gazed at the white crocheted duvet on the bed, and immediately wanted to sit at the pretty vanity and enjoy the beauty of the room. "Thank you, Fiona."

"No. Thank *you*," Galen said, as he stepped past them in the hall, continuing on to another room. He grinned back their way, then went inside, closing the door.

Rose blinked. If that was Galen's room, then they were less than twenty feet apart. She realized Fiona was watching her reaction, and Rose hurriedly said, "I'll drive to Tempest and get my things, then be back tonight, if that's all right."

"Fine, fine." Fiona beamed. "There's just one thing I should mention before you formally accept the job. And we'll all understand if you decide not to work here."

Rose wasn't about to turn away from this employment, not when it was everything she wanted, including having a big, handsome cowboy sleeping just feet away from her. "What is that?"

"We do ask, especially for the sake of the children, that you never go near the canyons, and that you never ride without an escort." Fiona looked sad about her words. "It's just the way it has to be for the sake of liability and the protection of our employees."

"That's fine," Rose said. "I completely understand."

The older woman beamed. "That's it, then. I'll let Jace go over the paperwork with you. Mealtimes are posted in the kitchen, as is what's being served."

Rose glanced one last time at the door Galen had passed through. All the Callahans had been rumored to be hard to tame—but once tamed, they made wonderful husbands and fathers.

If any man needed taming, it was Galen Callahan.

ROSE'S EYES SNAPPED OPEN in the night and she pulled the crocheted duvet up to her throat, telling herself she was nervous for no reason. She'd gone home and retrieved her things, and her father had sent her off full of dire warnings: Don't go anyplace by yourself, and don't let any of the Callahan men turn your head. They were rascals and scoundrels, and loved women like bees loved honey.

Her dad had no idea how much the thought of a rascal Callahan appealed to her. But the other warnings had scared her a bit. She'd heard tales of the danger that circled Rancho Diablo.

The door eased open, and she held her breath.

"Knock, knock," she heard a man's voice say softly.

"Yes?" At least it was a friendly visitor.

"It's Jace. Got a second?"

Rose wondered if this was a Callahan ritual. "Do you always make nocturnal visits?"

"Sometimes. Depends. She's in here, Galen. She says we can come in."

She hadn't said anything of the sort, but since Galen was around, Rose pushed herself eagerly to a sitting position. "What's going on?" she asked, flipping on the tiny lamp on her nightstand. "Oh, my goodness! What did you do to yourself?"

Both men were covered in mud from head to toe.

"Don't you dare get near my bed!" The pretty white coverlet wouldn't stand mud on it—she'd never get it out. "Step on that rug, and don't either of you move!" She hopped out of bed and pulled a robe from her closet, putting it on over her smiley-face pajamas.

Galen grinned at her. "Cute."

"Thanks." She wished she was wearing something sexier than the pajamas she'd had for the past two years, but she hadn't expected two handsome cowboys to visit her in her bedroom. "What have you been into?"

"We want you to come down to the canyons with us," Galen said. "We need a small, delicate person like you to do something."

Rose eyed the mud that covered their jeans and smudged their handsome faces. "You two are nothing but trouble, I can tell. It's written all over you."

"That's what they say," Jace said, and he looked so pleased about it that Rose wondered if either of these men could be tamed. She looked carefully at Galen.

"If I come with you, and I'm not saying I will, what is it that you want me to do? Because I don't want to come back looking like you. I don't think crawling around in canyons was in the employment contract I signed."

"We'll give you combat pay," Jace said. "Fiona baked fresh chocolate chip cookies tonight. You'll think you've died and gone to heaven."

"I bet. Occasionally, my dad sends me to Diablo to the Books'n'Bingo Society tearoom for cookies. We have a bakery in Tempest, but Dad likes what your aunt and her friends make better." Their cookies were lures, and the Callahans had other lures, too. Her gaze longingly touched on Galen's biceps, his broad chest, his lean hips in blue jeans.

Even caked in mud, he was so sexy she ached.

"So anyway," Rose said, "I assume this outing is dress-down?"

"Something a little less bright than smiley faces," Galen said cheerfully, and his brother glared at him.

"We'll step out while you change," Jace said, dragging him from the room.

Rose dressed quickly. Even though it was June, it could be cool in the canyons. She pulled on jeans she wouldn't mind getting filthy, a dark sweatshirt that read *Dark Shadows,* boots and a dark hat.

Galen's gaze widened when she joined them in the hall.

"I didn't expect you to wait on me right outside my door."

"Expediency," Galen said. "We're nothing if not expedient. *Dark Shadows?*"

She closed her door. "Seemed appropriate. You do go to the movies on occasion, don't you?"

"No, he doesn't go to the movies. He barely leaves this ranch. Galen is our resident nerd. Brother, it was also a black-and-white TV show many, many moons ago." Jace waved them down the stairs. She followed, and Galen brought up the rear.

"I'm not a nerd," he said, his deep voice husky. "I'm busy. And we didn't have televisions in the tribe. Not back then. I missed the good days of black-and-white TV."

"Don't mind him," Jace said, leading them through the kitchen. He slid all the cookies off the plate Fiona had put out and into a bag, and left the empty dish on the counter. "He's harmless. Some of us had the opportunity to watch television shows, but Galen was always studying."

They went out the kitchen door and headed to a truck. Rose was thrilled to be in on a Callahan caper. Their adventures were legendary; people spoke of their stories in reverent tones. Despite her father's warnings, she wouldn't have missed this for the world.

The brothers sandwiched her between them in the front seat, and she enjoyed the feeling of having a strong man seated on either side of her. "So what am I supposed to do?"

"We're going to lower you into a cave," Galen said. "We want you to tell us what's down there."

Bats and snakes, no doubt. "A cave?"

"Yeah. We've both tried, but we're too big to get inside, with only one of us to pull the other out." Galen winked. "We can lower you in and pull you out so fast it'll feel like you're on a carnival ride."

"Pretty sure she'll feel more like she's a puppet," Jace said. "With you being the puppeteer. Hope you're a better puppeteer than you are a TV trivia expert."

"I…" She wasn't about to refuse, not when Galen's

blue eyes were smiling at her as if they shared a secret. He really was the most handsome man she'd ever seen.

"We looked for our sister," Jace groused, "but Ash can never be found when she's needed."

"Maybe she doesn't want to be put in a cave," Rose said.

"When Ash can't be found, it's because she's tracking Xav down." Galen sighed. "Anyway, you're thinner."

"More petite," Jace said, "like a boy."

Rose gasped. "I'm nothing like a boy, thank you!"

"I didn't mean that, exactly," Jace said hurriedly, and Galen laughed.

"You're beautiful," he said. "And my brother's a dunce. Don't listen to a word he says. He has zero idea how to talk to a woman. Anyone on the ranch will tell you so."

Rose felt a bit better, and her spirits lifted. Galen thought she was beautiful! That had to be a good sign— even if he did want to lower her into a dark cave on her first night at Rancho Diablo.

GALEN COULDN'T BELIEVE he'd talked the tiny blonde into a midnight adventure. His good fortune kept improving. And she felt so soft and dainty next to him. When he'd seen her in those silly happy face pajamas, his body had been hit with a lightning strike of sexual attraction. Desire, fierce and strong, had poured over him, stopping his breath.

The truck hit a rut and they all bounced. Rose flew into his side, and a breast brushed his arm, which he gallantly tried to ignore. "Whoa," he said, "you all right?"

"I'm fine." She smiled at him before quickly looking back out the window.

"Jace isn't our best driver. He gets behind a steering wheel and thinks he's at Daytona." Galen didn't want Rose to feel awkward about the accidental closeness they'd just shared—but his mind went right back to the tempting touch he'd just received courtesy of his brother's terrible driving.

He was so glad Jace was driving.

"Not true," Jace said. "In defense of myself, I'm such a good driver, I could teach driver's education."

Rose smiled. "I'm sure you could, Jace."

A fire smoldered inside Galen, lit when he'd felt Rose's breast against his arm. What he wouldn't give to make that accidental touch the real thing. "Here's the turn, Jace."

He eyed the canyons, which were steeped in darkness. Somewhere out there, no doubt, their uncle Wolf's henchmen lurked. No one knew yet how the fire had started, but according to the sheriff, the quaint, solitary farmhouse on the neighboring land had burned to the ground. Fortunately, the foreman hadn't been home. Hadn't lived on the property, except for weekends, after he'd sold out to Storm Cash.

"This isn't Rancho Diablo, is it?" Rose asked.

"No," Galen said. "This is Rancho Not."

"Rancho Not?"

"What my ham-headed brother means," Jace said, "is that we're trespassing."

Rose glanced at Galen. "Why?"

"Because we're spying," he said simply. "Actually, we're not even spying. We're gathering intel."

"Spying," Rose said. "You think your uncle Wolf has planted something in the cave we're going to."

"Not just another pretty face," Jace said. "You see,

Galen, I told you she had brains as well as beauty. You said Rose was a looker, and I said she was also a brain."

"You were focused on my superficialities and not my intelligence?" Rose asked Galen.

"That's about the size of it," Jace said, happy to have him land in hot water with a huge splash. "This is the spot. Let me help you out, dollface."

Galen glowered at his brother, who ignored his obvious discomfort with his flirting. "Dollface" took Jace's hand, and he helped her from the truck, leaving Galen with no option except to get out and tag along behind them with a Maglite and a case of unexpected jealousy.

He had no reason to feel jealous. He barely knew Rose, and Jace was a boob of epic proportion. Rose would never be interested in his wild-eyed brother. *And anyway, I have no place in my life for a girlfriend. Even one as sexy as Rose.*

"Galen, tie the rope around Rose. I'll check for snakes and bats, one last time."

She let out an involuntary squeal. Galen grinned as he wrapped the rope around her tiny waist. "Don't listen to him. He just likes to hear you squeak."

"Well, I will, and loudly if there's anything down there with two eyes!" Rose watched with trepidation as Jace shone his own Maglite into the crevice. "How did you ever find this cave?"

"Our intel revealed that there's a lot of activity around this location. Then we found this cave. We want to know what's down there." Galen pulled the rope taut, tugging her a little closer to him. She smelled good, a flowery scent that tantalized him. "I'll be at the other end of this rope, and nothing will happen to you. If you want to come out, you just jerk it, and we'll get you out faster than a genie out of a bottle."

"You'd better," Rose warned. "Or I'll commandeer the bag of cookies and not give you a single one."

"That's my girl," Jace said, "hit him where it hurts. Now down you go."

Galen handed her a flashlight, then stepped close to the edge of the cave opening, shining his own light so they could see as she was lowered down.

"What exactly am I looking for?" she asked, glancing up.

"Bodies," Jace said. "Dead bodies."

She let out a small gasp.

Galen laughed. "Don't frighten her."

"That's right." Jace grinned at Rose as he let out more rope. "You're like a canary," he told her. "You're going to let us know if there's any trouble down below."

"Canaries die," Rose said.

Galen smiled, impressed with her spirit. "Only in the case of noxious gas. And believe me, I'm up here with the only noxious gas around. You're just going to be down there for a moment." His words seemed to soothe her, but Galen felt suddenly anxious as Rose disappeared from sight.

It got very quiet underneath the velvety New Mexico sky. Galen listened, his pulse thundering, his breath short, his stomach even cramping a bit—maybe he shouldn't have allowed his brother to talk him into this— and then suddenly, the rope went completely slack.

Chapter Three

"Rose!" Galen shouted, realizing that she was no longer at the end of the rope he held. He tossed it away, as did his brother. The two of them flattened themselves against the lip of the cave, peering down. "Rose!"

"Hold your horses," she called from below. "All that bellowing is making me nervous."

"What are you doing?" Galen gulped against the fear tightening his throat. She sounded as if she was talking to them from the bottom of a jar. "You were supposed to just take a quick look and come back out."

"Yeah, but it's pretty cool down here."

Galen shone the flashlight into the crevice. "Put the rope back on and get up here!"

"Keep your pants on, boys. I may never come this way again, so I want to fully live in the moment."

"What the hell is she doing?" Jace muttered. They pressed as close as they could to the hole, trying in vain to see what Rose was up to.

"I know just as much as you do, which isn't exactly a comforting feeling," Galen said.

"She's a sparky little thing, isn't she?" Jace commented, his tone admiring.

"Don't you have a girlfriend?" Galen demanded.

"Not to my knowledge. Sometimes I wish I did. Other times, I think how lucky I am that there's no nagging woman in my life."

"Hey!" Rose called up. "I heard that! I think you should know it's a well-known fact that men nag as much as women. Sometimes more. Now, get your muscles going, fellows. I'm ready to come out."

Galen grabbed the rope with relief. He and Jace tugged her out as fast as they prudently could. She came out of the crevice, illuminating herself with the Maglite.

"Look," she said. "I'm Tinkerbell, rising from Hook's lantern."

"Someone likes children," Jace said. "Which is a fortunate thing, because I like children myself. Maybe you and I—" they set Rose on solid ground "—should think about having some children of our own."

"I don't think so," she said sweetly, and she smiled at Galen, whose breath went out of him. "Anyway, look at what I found." She held up a handful of silver coins, jingling them.

He was about to say, *Marvelous, but you had me so worried when the rope went slack,* when the sound of a truck engine approaching sent them running for their own truck.

"Holy crap," Jace said, patting his jeans. "Where are the keys?"

"Damn it!" Galen exclaimed as they sat breathlessly watching Jace look frantically for the keys.

"Those keys on the dash?" Rose asked, and Galen uttered a curse word he never thought he'd say in a lady's presence. Jace grabbed them and jammed one into the ignition.

"Wait!" Rose said. "We probably left a ton of footprints. They'll know we were here!"

"No time to clean that up. Floor it, Jace." Galen looked behind them. "Unknown vehicle at six o'clock."

Jace switched on the engine, pulling away from the cave without turning on the truck lights. They sped into the darkness, and Galen lifted a rifle down from the gun rack, watching behind them.

Once they made it to the main road, he let out a ragged breath. "I don't think they saw us."

"Or decided not to give chase," Jace said.

"It's beautiful down there," Rose said, completely unbothered by their haphazard getaway. "You can't believe all the amazing stuff in that cave." She held up the coins, eyeing them in the beam of her flashlight. "And look at this awesome statue."

Galen stared at the delicate silver figure of a mustang, a Diablo, in Rose's even more delicate palm. "That's Rancho Diablo treasure."

"Really?" Rose handed it over and he took it, reverently touching the horse, feeling it hum with the spirit that kept Rancho Diablo alive. "Then you're going to love this, too." She reached into her waistband and pulled out a handgun, giving that to him.

"What were you doing down there? Excavating?" Jace demanded. "Next time, we'll send you with a sack so you can bring up everything your heart desires."

"Good," Rose said, "because I had to leave behind a really sweet painting of your grandfather."

Galen stared at the woman sitting next to him, the new nanny they'd hired to watch the children and educate them and play with them, and it hit him that he was in the presence of a kindred spirit. A spirit that was unafraid and that walked in harmony with each moment. "How do you know it was our grandfather?"

She looked at him. "Everyone in Tempest knows Chief Running Bear. He hangs out sometimes at the Ice Cream Shoppe. You've got property in Tempest, so when he's in town, he stops by. The kids love his stories." She was quiet for a moment, then said, "I took some photos on my cell phone. I'll be very curious to see if this Maglite gave off enough light to capture anything. Too bad you can't fit down there. It's like a museum of contraband."

Galen's breath caught at her sheer bravery, not to mention audacity. Instead of worrying that she'd barely escaped detection and possibly danger, Rose acted as if she'd passed a pleasant evening in an enchanted grotto. She handed him a cookie from the bag, and gave one to Jace, too. Then she smiled at Galen, and he grinned back, abruptly aware that his heart had just jumped headlong into the hands of a woman who wore smiley-face pajamas to bed.

GALEN LAY IN HIS BED after a hot shower, unable to wipe the smile off his face. He'd looked at the photos Rose had taken of the cave, and with the powerful Maglite she'd been able to illuminate some revealing items. There was a cache of guns in the hole, enough to do great damage in the hands of some dedicated shooters. He'd share those photos at the emergency family meeting he planned to call tonight. The painting of his grandfather had been a bit more difficult to see, but it was still an amazing portrait of a man he couldn't imagine sitting still long enough to be painted.

Galen resolved to get that painting out of the cave

ASAP. It looked as if they'd been using his grandfather's likeness for the purposes of recognition and training. No doubt Wolf—or the cartel—had a bounty on Running Bear's head. The portrait was old, done maybe twenty-five years ago—hard to tell without seeing it in good light—and no doubt stolen. Galen wasn't certain how many years had passed since Wolf and Running Bear's relationship had ruptured forever, but maybe Wolf had taken the portrait when he'd left the tribe.

Galen would be willing to bet his uncle also had photos or sketches of the four elder Callahans the cartel wanted flushed out for turning them over to the government: Molly and Jeremiah Callahan, his cousins' parents, who'd built up this ranch, and Julia and Carlos Chacon Callahan, his and his siblings' parents, who'd wholeheartedly embraced the battle for Rancho Diablo. Wolf would never stop trying to turn the Callahans over to the cartel, but they were in hiding, in witness protection. They'd never be found.

No one knew where they were, not even Fiona.

No one except Running Bear.

And me. But I've kept myself away from anything that might weaken me for so long, I know that secret is buried deep within me. I don't understand Wolf's desire for vengeance on his family. Even if they turned him in to the government, he shouldn't want his relatives dead.

Family is all that matters.

Galen glanced over at the silver horse standing on his nightstand. The filigreed saddle glinted in the moonlight pouring in his bedroom window. It was a fine piece, designed by a master silversmith.

The mustang had come from someone who knew the old ways, and who understood the Diablos.

There was only one person he could think of who knew such things: his father, Carlos.

Somehow, Wolf had gotten hold of it, which meant he was getting closer. Galen decided he would wait until morning to discuss the situation with Grandfather, and then proceed with a family meeting. Matters were turning urgent.

An almost silent tap on his door interrupted his raging thoughts. "Yes?"

The door opened. "Galen?" Rose said. "Can I come in?"

"Sure." He sat up, turned on the lamp on his bedside table. "What's wrong?"

"Nothing." She sat on the foot of his bed, wrapped in a plaid red-and-green robe that didn't match the smiley-face pajamas she'd put back on. She wore some kind of fuzzy boots that looked comfortable and warm, and her blond hair had been washed clean of dirt and cobwebs, hanging in damp strands around her scrubbed, makeup-free face.

He thought she was cute as a baby deer.

"I forgot to tell you something else I saw in the cave."

"What?"

"Besides the weapons," Rose said, "there was also a front loader. I didn't take a photo, because it was at the back." Her blue eyes focused directly on him, waiting for him to draw the same conclusion she had.

"A front loader."

She nodded.

Galen leaned back against the wall, his arms crossed over his bare chest. "There's no way they got a big piece of machinery down the crevice, and filled the spot back in. The ground we were lying on was solid."

"Exactly."

Suddenly, Wolf's desire to keep them off the new property became clear—and Storm's wish to sell them the land because "things were happening there he wasn't comfortable with" made more sense.

"They've dug a damn tunnel," Galen said. "They're burrowing under Rancho Diablo and the land across the canyons."

"Could come from as far away as Mexico," Rose agreed. "I think that cave is just a storeroom, an adjunct off the main tunnel. Maybe I went down some kind of air vent, or a fissure that's recently cracked open, which they haven't discovered. Had you ever noticed it before?"

Galen hadn't, and right now it was hard to think with Rose sitting on his bed, a vision of temptation. What he wanted to do was grab her and kiss her, maybe even find out what was under those happy-face pajamas. But one didn't seduce an employee, no matter how sexy she was.

His brothers had seduced employees and made them wives.

Not me. I'm going to leave well enough alone. We shouldn't even have sent her down an air vent or shaft or whatever the hell that stupid hole was. What was I thinking?

He'd been thinking that he wanted any excuse at all to see her, and hadn't dreamed she'd accept this mission and throw herself into it with more gusto than any Callahan.

"We haven't had a whole lot of chances to check out that land. First of all, it's huge, so there's a lot to cover. We don't have the manpower to do it, especially when we'd be trespassing." Galen rubbed his shoulder absently. "But Xav Phillips was over there poking around one day—he's one of our foremen—and he noticed something funny about the ground in that area."

"We should go back and check it out more thoroughly, maybe in daylight."

He looked at her, stunned. "You sound way too much like my sister. Don't even think about going back there without me."

Rose smiled, and his slow-working brain went blank as he stared at her mouth. Those lips were just made for him to kiss. He could feel it, the call of the wild screaming through his blood.

"I won't," she said, and he snapped back to the present.

"I'll fire you if you do, on the spot, no questions asked," he warned, suddenly afraid that Rose was indeed just like his sister, with an impetuous, adventuresome nature that bordered on wildness.

Or bravery. The military would call it bravery.

His sister was too brave for her own good. And this spunky woman on the end of his bed was beginning to sound very much the same.

"I promise," Rose said. "It wouldn't be any fun without you, anyway."

"I wouldn't call what we did tonight fun."

She smiled again. "It was a lot of fun."

"You realize we were within a rabbit's foot of getting shot at."

"You had us covered. I trust your marksmanship."

Galen closed his eyes for just a moment, opening them to stare at her. In the photo she'd snapped of the weapons cache, there'd been a few AK-47s, and a few more exotic styles of weaponry. Someone was gearing up for battle, and he wondered if Rose recognized just how little protection his rifle would have been against, say, a clip with multiple rounds in it. "While my marksmanship is decent, we didn't want to get caught."

"That's true." Rose stood, her look teasing. "Still, it was something to tell the grandkids, wasn't it?"

He shook his head. "God, no. Monkey hear, monkey do. Didn't you ever tell your parents, 'Well, you did it, why can't I?' As far as the kids are concerned, one should never admit to anything more than sitting in church seven days a week. At least that's my plan."

Rose laughed. "Not a very believable one, but whatever. When you have kids, you can revise your strategy." She went to the door. "Good night, Galen."

He watched her disappear into the hallway. When the door closed, he turned off the lamp and tried to settle back into a relaxed state conducive to sleeping.

It wasn't going to work. Between the tale of the tunnel under Rancho Diablo, and the sweet woman he knew was sleeping just down the hall, Galen wasn't certain he would ever relax again.

His phone buzzed with an incoming text. He glanced at it, his gaze widening with each word.

You know a tunnel under Rancho Diablo means this ranch is sitting on Dante's Inferno? And maybe the nine circles of Hell? You should let me go down there again to find the entrance. I just need a little more time and equipment. If there's a tunnel, it's reinforced, so it would be a great find to turn over to the local authorities.

Galen's blood chilled. Rose would do it. She wouldn't think anything about turning over information about what she'd found to the sheriff, or probably even to the government. He thought he remembered hearing that her father had been in the military in a secret division, and then was a Texas Ranger before being voted Tempest's sheriff many years ago.

Mr. Carstairs had spawned a fighter.

Nothing good could come of such a darling girl with the genes of a warrior sitting in her bed, pondering the next phase of an adventure she was itching to ignite.

Then again, there was no reason the two of them couldn't ignite things together. Why start a fire by yourself when you could invite a friend to create mayhem with you?

Galen jumped out of bed, tossed on a T-shirt and jeans and headed down the hall.

Chapter Four

Rose raised a brow as Galen tore through her bedroom door. "Well, hello. Come to tell me what a great idea I had?"

"No," he said, surprising her by hopping under the covers with her. "I've come to put my cold feet on you, which you richly deserve, after writing me that nonsense. And if you think I'm going to argue with you by text, you're badly mistaken. Now turn off the light, and let's talk this out."

She complied as he got comfortable under the duvet. "You do have cold feet."

"Remember that," Galen said. "Cold feet, warm heart."

"So I hear." They lay side by side in the dark. "I don't usually have a cowboy jump in my bed, so I'm not sure what the standard protocol is, but do you want a cookie, and maybe a sip of hot tea? It's not as hot as it was, because I was down in your room, but it's still good." She reached into the bag on her nightstand and offered him a cookie. "I've developed an addiction to your aunt's baking."

"No cookie. No tea. You're changing the subject, trying to get my mind off your text with some sugary lures."

"Maybe." She sipped her tea in the darkness, loving the feel of the big, strong man tucked up next to her in bed. She could definitely get used to this. "I'm right."

"But you won't go through with it on your own."

She sighed. "Just think about my plan for a few days. You've got to find out what's happening under your own ranch."

"You won't tell a soul," Galen said. "Not Ash, not Jace, not Fiona, not anyone."

"Of course I won't. It's your ranch, your family." She put her teacup back down. "I always dreamed of having a room like this."

"Didn't you have a girlie room?"

"Sort of girlie. Not very. My mom died when I was very young."

"I'm sorry," Galen murmured.

"I was, too." Rose took a deep breath. "Anyway, after college I began a busy job at a financial planning company. Didn't have time to girlie up my room. Lived in a square box in Manhattan with no closet to speak of." She laughed. "I look back on those days with a smile, because I learned a lot. This room is a treat."

"You got me off the subject again."

"You asked. Anyway, I already swore myself to silence. Your secret is totally safe."

"All right. Then I'll head back to my own bed and leave you to your snack."

She giggled. "Fiona says she's baking gingerbread tomorrow. I'm going to get fat."

"I very much doubt it. But a pound or two will only enhance those great curves you've got going on."

The man was born to flirt. She tried not to take it too seriously, decided to turn the topic back to business.

"You know, if I quit eating Fiona's treats, I can easily fit back through that opening—"

"No. If anybody goes back down in that hole, it's going to be a Callahan. Maybe Ashlyn."

"You wouldn't put your sister in danger," Rose said. "That much I know about you already. In fact, you won't even want your sister to know it's there."

"A truer statement was never spoken in this room." He got out of bed. "See you at breakfast."

"Bye," Rose said, catching a glimpse of his physique as he passed the window. He was a scrumptious hunk of man, and she should tempt him to stay longer. "Good night."

"Good night."

He closed the door, and Rose leaned back in bed. She put the cookies down, drank the rest of her tea and then got up to brush her teeth. The cookies *had* been a sugary lure, as Galen had noted.

Tomorrow, gingerbread.

GALEN DIDN'T GET much sleep, but then again, sleep wasn't at the forefront of his mind. The gaping problem they'd unearthed last night deeply concerned him.

In the morning, he went to the canyons to try to root out his grandfather. Running Bear sat at the fire ring, the stone circle where he'd brought them when they'd first arrived at Rancho Diablo. The chief had told the Chacon Callahan siblings that this was now their new home.

Galen loved this land.

"Chief," he said, and the old man seated on the ground, eyes closed, face raised to the sky, nodded.

"When you have a moment, I need to pick your brains."

"I have many moments."

Galen seated himself on the earth next to his grandfather, felt the spring sun warm his skin. "There is no place like Rancho Diablo."

"There are many spirits here. Mother Earth is strong and beautiful in this place."

"But there's a bad current running under her, Grandfather."

"I know."

Galen sighed. His grandfather was always one step ahead of them, and knew the beginning, middle and maybe even the end of the journey they were on. Running Bear had also warned the siblings that one of them was the hunted one, the one who would bring danger to the family. Sometimes Galen wondered if it was him. He'd rather it was, than any of his siblings. One day they would know—and no doubt the decision they would face would be difficult.

Today, he had to worry about trouble closer to home. "The enemy may have built reinforced tunnels under our ranch." He looked into the distance, seeing the deep canyons and mesas that time had carved into the land. "We found some machinery in a cave. The only explanation is that it's at the beginning of a tunnel, or underground bunkers. They could be right underneath the house."

"I know." Running Bear rested his palms on his knees. "They are not there. Yet."

"But they're coming."

"They are. It's their mission."

"To what purpose?" Galen pulled his cowboy hat lower, shielding his face from the sun.

"To surround us. If they can do that, they'll have a stranglehold here that will be hard to break."

"How do we stop them? Make sure they don't get here?"

"Buy the land from Storm."

Galen considered that. They'd need a consortium of some kind to buy that much land without stretching the resources of Rancho Diablo. "We'll be operating on limited manpower."

"We'll hire more people. Or bring the Callahan cousins home. Let them live here, where there are no tunnels. One of you would have had the land eventually, if you'd won Fiona's raffle."

"We always figured that was a fairy tale you guys cooked up to get us married and with families."

"No," Running Bear said. "Well, yes and no. Yes, Fiona will do anything to see you happy, as your married cousins and siblings are. But we always intended to grow the ranch. We knew they were building tunnels. We hoped you would come to love it here as much as your cousins do."

"I do. The whole family does."

"I know. But one of you must be the head of that ranch. We don't want it broken up and weakened, making it easy for the cartel to move in."

Galen shook his head. "I don't like it. If Ash wins the ranch, she'll be over there alone. She may not want us all living there. We need to stay together as a family. As a unit. We always have."

"So win the land yourself."

"I have no reason to expect that I'm in the running. I have no wife, probably won't for years." He'd taken care of his siblings so long he didn't know if he'd ever be able to relax and have time for romance.

He thought about Rose next to him in bed last night and decided he could relax a little.

"Tell your brothers and sister that you want the land."

Galen started. "I can't do that. I can't tell them I'm bumping them out of Fiona's ploy."

"You don't want any of them living on land that only you knows has been compromised. It's not safe."

"Can't we destroy the tunnels?"

"We would destroy acres and acres of good land with them."

There were no good answers, no good choices. "It's too dangerous to raise a family there now, so what difference would it make if we destroyed it? Those tunnels are how they're getting to Rancho Diablo so easily, Grandfather."

"Yes." Running Bear nodded. "You must ask your ancestors what the right answer is."

"The right answer to what?"

"Your path. What you are meant to do."

"I say we burn them out. From burned ground comes new growth."

"It would take many men to do it."

That was also true. He'd had lots of military training. Teamwork wasn't unknown to him. "It would be expensive to bring in that much personnel."

"Yes. But it can't be done alone."

"Explosives. I can think of a hundred ways to collapse tunnels."

His grandfather opened his eyes to look at him. "You'd be put in jail. You can't set fires and blow up land without breaking the law."

"There has to be a way." Galen just couldn't think of one. But it made his blood hot with anger that the enemy was gaining on them by doing whatever they wanted, while he was confined by the law. "Some way I haven't thought of yet."

"Buy the land," Running Bear advised. "Tell Storm you will."

"By myself? Or you mean the family as a conglomerate?"

"You buy the land. Tell your cousins you need to use the resources of Rancho Diablo as collateral. Jonas Callahan will know what you need."

The treasure of Rancho Diablo. Galen knew about it. There were a couple working oil wells, the fabled silver mine, the buried silver and gold, as well as the land and its holdings. But the black Diablo mustangs were the real wealth. They held the spirit of the land, kept it alive. "What does Wolf think he wants with Rancho Diablo?"

"The wealth. The riches." Running Bear rose. "What my son does not understand is that he cannot have any of those things. They will never be his."

Galen rose with his grandfather. "How is that?"

"Because evil never overcomes good. This ranch was built for good. The fight will be long. It will be difficult and costly. But it will not be lost. Think on what I have said, Galen." His grandfather looked at him. "Tell Fiona the terms of the ranch raffle must change, if she's going to get the last of you boys, and even Ash, to the altar."

"Change how? And I don't want to get married," Galen said. "I've been alone too long. I like my life the way it is."

"The shepherd must eventually have a flock." Running Bear walked toward the gorges twisting through rocks carved by eons of wind and rain.

"I don't need a flock," Galen muttered. "And I don't

need a twenty-thousand acre ranch." He sighed as he got in the jeep. "I don't want the land. I want to burn them out," he called after his grandfather. "Let the rest of them divide up the ranch over there."

Silence met his words. Which meant the old chief had said all he planned to say on the matter.

Running Bear knew what had to happen.

Galen went back to Rancho Diablo to think.

SOMER STEVENS MET HIM as he drove up to the ranch house, a big smile on her face. "Just the man I was hoping to see."

He parked the jeep, appreciating her dark beauty. And yet somehow she just didn't ring his bell the way Rose did. "Why is that?"

"Wondered if you want to go riding. I'm fixing to take out Gray."

"I'm afraid I can't join you today," Galen said, and wondered why she rubbed him the wrong way. Maybe because she was a shade too friendly.

"Next time, perhaps." She disappeared into the barn, and Galen stared after her. He hoped she planned to exercise Gray in the corralled area of the ranch, where it was safest. What if it were Rose riding? Would she stay near the house, or stray off on an adventure?

Definitely stray off, for any reason.

Somer wasn't his problem. She was Sloan and Kendall's problem. She'd been hired to take Sawyer's place guarding their twins. Occasionally she would switch and guard Tighe and River's triplets. If she had an afternoon off, it wasn't his business.

He went inside the house, his mind full of his grandfather's advice.

"Hello!" Fiona grinned at him. "Why is your smile turned upside down, nephew?"

He sat at the kitchen counter, nodding gratefully when she pushed a mug of coffee and a slice of apple pie his way. "Thank you. Running Bear wants me to buy the ranch across the canyons," he said, and bit into the deep, flaky pastry. Cinnamon and allspice and warm buttery piecrust melted in his mouth.

"You?" Fiona looked at him curiously.

He shrugged.

"Why?"

He couldn't tell her everything. That was Running Bear's job. Those two had been thick as thieves forever. "He's got some plan working. But he said you needed better bait to get the rest of us married off. The ranch land plan isn't going to work. I might remind you I don't see myself as exactly marriage bound. Nor does Jace. Ashlyn is a wild card. I wouldn't put too much of your pin money on that horse."

He'd paraphrased Running Bear's words, but it would indeed take more than land to get him to the altar.

Unless Rose was available. Maybe I'd consider it then.

"That was my best lure!" Fiona exclaimed. "How do I come up with a better prize than a ranch, I ask you?" His tiny aunt looked ruffled and annoyed. "Running Bear has some nerve, changing horses midstream." She sat down in a huff on the stool next to Galen's.

"No one really understands the workings of the chief's mind, do they?" He took another bite of pie, giving a sigh of appreciation. "Your apple pie is the best, Aunt Fiona."

She made an impatient noise. "Don't butter me up,

nephew. You do realize the fly in your grandfather's horse pucky ointment?"

"There's usually a lot of flies involved in what either of you do. I keep a flyswatter handy."

"Your siblings will resent you, dare I say even want to string you up, if you buy the ranch land and put them out of the raffle." Fiona's face wore a studious, concerned frown. "You're a strong man, but not strong enough to be scorned and ostracized by the family you raised."

His aunt spoke the unvarnished truth. "What can I do?"

"I don't know. Your grandfather is leaving me holding the proverbial bag, too. What am I going to tell your siblings? I set all of you up for marriage and families, and now you get nada?" Fiona looked as if she might cry. "I think there's some law against bait-and-switch tactics like the ones your grandfather is proposing. Where is he, anyway? I want to give him a piece of my mind. No more chocolate chip cookies for him!"

Galen shrugged. "I guess I'll head to the bank and start working up funding. First I'll need to talk to Storm and make certain he understands I'm not going to pay a king's ransom for land he just bought and never worked. Not to mention that the only livable dwelling just burned to the ground."

"Oh, that termite pile should have been razed a long time ago," Fiona said, sounding crankier than he'd ever heard her. "The land itself is the only thing of value there."

Land with a maze of tunnels dug by dangerous smugglers running under it. "It's not just me my sibs are going to be annoyed with. They love their families, but they're going to think you planned this all along."

She gasped. "I did no such thing! Running Bear is off his rocker! I can't be responsible for your grandfather's deviations. I'm just the handler around here. And most of the time it's like herding feral cats, I can tell you." She went off, highly annoyed. Galen grinned and finished his pie.

Rose came in and took Fiona's chair. "Howdy, stranger."

He looked at her, his whole being suddenly filled with happiness for some stupid reason. Why this woman affected him this way he couldn't quite put his finger on. Yes, she was cute, adorable, even. Had a sparky personality, and was brave as a tiger. Had sexy curves he'd love to get to know. But that wasn't enough to get his engine revving in overdrive every time he saw her, was it?

Who am I kidding? It's more than enough. I'm about to break into a cold sweat just looking at her.

"Fiona made apple pie. Want a slice?"

She shook her head. "No, thanks. I'm going riding with Somer in a bit."

He hesitated. "Somer?"

"Yes. Why?" Rose gave him a curious look. "Something wrong with that?"

"No. Nothing at all. Just weren't aware the two of you were on such friendly terms."

She smiled. "We're the two new girls. Gives us a bond."

"Oh. I see."

"Yes. But then again, I'm on friendly terms with everyone."

He could believe that. Even he tended toward more-than-monosyllabic when Rose was around. "You girls just checking out the scenery?"

"I did that last night with you." She winked at him, and his stomach gave a little twist. Which was dumb, because women didn't usually make him nervous.

This one did.

"Anyway," Rose said, "we're doing a little training."

"Training?"

"You know, horse training. Get them a little more acclimated to Rancho Diablo."

He stared at Rose, wishing he could kiss her. He couldn't, of course. She was a ranch employee.

He'd been in her bed last night, and he'd liked it—even if not a darn thing had happened.

"Somer knows a lot about horses. Apparently, she and Sawyer grew up near each other, and both of them—"

"What?" Galen asked, tearing his concentration away from Rose's lips with supreme effort. "What do you mean, Somer and Sawyer grew up near each other?"

"They're cousins," Rose said. "Didn't you know?"

An uneasy feeling came over him. "They can't be. That would have had to be disclosed on the ranch application." Now that he thought about it, he recalled that Fiona had been in charge of reviewing the applications and making appointments for interviews.

Rose smiled at him. "I don't like spilling beans. I better get a slice of pie before my mouth gets me in trouble."

He'd like to get her mouth in trouble. Galen shook his head and carried his dish to the sink. "Feel free to spill anytime. I'm on my way into town to do some bank paperwork. And about last night..." he said, turning to face her.

"I know. Not a word. I wouldn't tell a soul." She smiled, and he grinned back, unable to help responding to the mischief in her eyes.

"No, what I was going to say is that we probably shouldn't have sent you down in that cave. It was a terrible idea. I shouldn't have let Jace talk me into it."

"Oh, so he's the adventurous brother. I'll keep that in mind." She bit into her pie. "You have no idea how lucky you are that your aunt Fiona bakes and cooks. Home cooking is a luxury."

"Well, she's annoyed right now, so if we get dinner, it'll be a miracle."

"Annoyed?" Rose raised a brow. "Did you make her mad?"

"Somewhat. I guess so." He sighed. "Because of what we found, I'm going to buy Storm's land."

"All on your own?"

He nodded, glad to have someone to tell about it.

"You're going to be the black sheep in your family," Rose said, laughing. "Jace told me that if Sawyer hadn't disappeared, he might have talked her into a fake marriage just so he could get his ticket in to win the ranch."

"That would be cheating."

Rose put her plate down, poured them each a glass of tea. "Not cheating. Maximizing his chances."

"Cheating." Galen took a sip. "Jace told you that?"

"Sure. Just like your sister told me that she's gone off Xav Phillips."

He choked on the tea, set the glass down. "Gone off? As in isn't trying to herd him to the altar anymore?"

"I guess not." Rose looked thoughtful. "So maybe the field is completely clear for you now, after all."

"Why does everybody tell you everything? I should know these things."

"Maybe I'm a little easier to talk to you than you are?" she teased. "Or they don't want to let big brother down."

"It's still no reason to make you the resident advice columnist," Galen groused. He was thunderstruck by everything he'd learned. "Does Somer know where Sawyer's gone? Or why she left?"

"No. Didn't say anything to me about it. I'd better go, though. Don't want to keep her waiting." She put her plate in the dishwasher.

"Just a minute," Galen said, wishing she would stay a little longer. "Anything else I need to know?"

Rose smiled. "Perhaps."

"I'm listening." He wanted to kiss her in the worst way. Hopefully, he didn't look like his brothers had when they'd been all slobbery about the women who were now their wives. That was the thing about watching his siblings fall like rocks to the bottom of a well—the process had been ugly.

He sure didn't want to do ugly. "I'm listening, if there's something I should know."

"Here's something you should know," Rose said. Then to Galen's utter astonishment, she walked over and pressed her lips against his in a gentle kiss that happened so quickly he didn't have time to pucker up. She went out the back door, leaving him glued to the floor, his whole body humming like a divining rod.

She'd just kissed him. She wanted him to know she liked him—that could be her only meaning. And he'd missed the moment, like a giant doofus stuck on stupid. Hadn't even kissed her back, or put a hand on her to drag her close to him. The way he would have if he hadn't been frozen with shock.

If she ever does that again, I'll pucker up like a girl

in a kissing booth. I won't be like my brothers. I'm not going down hard.

No, if that little gal wants me, I'm pretty sure I'll fold like a cheap seat at a picnic—fast and easy.

Chapter Five

The last thing Galen wanted to do was talk to Storm Cash, but thanks to his grandfather's directive he saw no reason to linger—even if he'd rather chase after Rose and find out if she had any more sugar with his name on it.

"Hi," Storm said, when Galen drove up in his truck and got out. "It's not often that I see a Callahan at my place. Is this a friendly call?"

"I hope so. It'll start out that way. Could go either direction, depending on the weather."

Storm laughed. "You Callahans are moody cusses, that's for certain. What's on your mind?"

"I may take you up on buying the land you offered us," he said without stalling.

Storm picked up a bale of hay and tossed it into his truck bed. "Might you?"

"Is the offer still open?"

"Sure it is. I'm not the kind of man to go back on my word."

Sometimes Storm seemed honest to his bones. Galen couldn't say why he and his siblings felt a sense of unease about the big man. They just did. But then again, they didn't trust many outsiders. "Why do you want to sell it? You didn't buy it that many moons ago."

"Let's just say that I'm uncomfortable with the undercurrents attached to that land."

That was a signal to dig deeper if he'd ever heard one. "Storm, you might as well get it off your chest. Skeletons don't go away, you know. They have a disturbing tendency to hang around and rattle when you least expect it."

"True," his neighbor said, "but it's not the skeletons I'm worried about."

"So it's the mercenaries," Galen stated, and Storm looked him straight in the eye.

"Look, I'll sell the land to you for a quarter less than I paid for it. I just want rid of it, Callahan. Take it or leave it."

Galen watched his expression carefully. Storm had less of a poker face than he might have imagined. The man seemed concerned about something. Galen decided to be the needle that dug out the splinter. "That's quite a loss you'll take on the asking price."

"I've got a beautiful fiancée. I don't have time to oversee an enormous ranch," Storm said.

"I think there's more to the story."

His neighbor gave him a dry look. "I don't want to get caught in the middle of anything."

"Nothing to get caught in the middle of. We're the good guys." A sudden thought occurred to Galen. "Wait a minute. You've come to our ranch a couple of times mentioning that you'd found stragglers camping on your land. That there were trespassers you couldn't control. You haven't been threatened in any way, have you?"

"If you want to buy the land across the canyons *and*

my land, you've got yourself a deal, neighbor. We'll leave it at that."

Galen blinked, caught off guard. "You planning to move away, Storm? You haven't been on this spread but about four or five years, have you?"

"Think I'll move into town, to Lu's place," Storm said evenly.

The rancher *had* been threatened. Galen's sixth sense was going wild with warning. "What does Lu think about that?"

Lu Feinstrom was Storm's lady friend. She was a great cook and quite a woman. Storm had gone down like a sack of hammers for her and her cooking.

"She'd rather live here. But what can I do?" He glanced at the sky. "Looks like a storm is coming, Callahan. I'm going to have to bring some livestock in. Have your lawyer or agent send me an offer. Then we'll smoke on it."

"I'll do that." Galen watched as the big man headed off in his truck, then got in his and drove back to Rancho Diablo.

"IT'S BEAUTIFUL, FIONA," Rose said, gazing at the wedding dress on her bed. "But I don't know anything about modeling wedding gowns."

"Sure you do," Fiona said brightly. "Just hop in that one and let's see what you see. I mean, let's see how it fits you."

"What is this big event Rancho Diablo is hosting?" Rose couldn't say why she didn't want to put the gown on, she just didn't.

On the other hand, she couldn't disappoint Fiona, whose face was bright and expectant.

"I'm just about out of bachelors, except for Jace," Fiona told her. "So this Christmas, for the Christmas ball, I'm going to do a bride-a-thon. Doesn't that sound like fun?"

"You're planning early." Rose's heart shifted a bit. "How can you be out of bachelors?"

"I just ran out of available options." Fiona snapped her fingers. "I can't raise enough money for the charity projects I'm working on by selling cookies and pies, you know. So this time I'm going to have a bride-a-thon to end all bride-a-thons."

Rose backed up a bit farther from the gorgeous gown. "What about Galen?"

"Oh, Galen's a pinhead and Jace is loosey-goosey. Couldn't get much for either of them. No, this year we're going for the bachelorette angle. Much more lucrative, I'll bet. Sure you don't want to try this on? It's still got the price tag attached."

Rose didn't think there could be anything more lucrative than Galen strutting on stage in front of a couple hundred leering ladies. "I bid on Galen year before last," she said. "I'd bid again."

Galen walked into her room just as the words left her mouth. He grinned and gave her a sly wink.

"I really appreciate that vote of confidence, doll face. I'm sorry you didn't win me. Maybe another time."

"I don't think so," Rose said. "Your aunt says you're unavailable."

Galen raised a brow. "Am I, aunt?"

"I think it's a terminal thing," Fiona muttered, gazing at the dress with some sadness. "I had great hopes for you and Jace, but the truth is, you two may be runts."

Rose laughed, the idea of this tall man being a runt too ludicrous to imagine. "Poor Galen."

He grabbed his aunt to him and gave her a big smooch on the cheek. She squealed and wriggled out of his arms. "Who's the victim that's going in that white shroud, aunt?"

"I was trying," Fiona said with some asperity, "to get Rose to put it on, but it seems she doesn't fancy white shrouds, as you so illustratively call this delightful creation." She sailed from the room, murmuring about needing to redo her victim list.

"I think I let her down."

"I wouldn't worry. My aunt will have another plot on her mind soon enough that she'll want to snare you in."

Galen smiled, and Rose felt her knees go slightly weak. She glanced at the gown again. "It's not really my style. I'm a little more casual, I think."

"I'm surprised at Fiona," Galen said, peering at the gown more closely. "This is from the shop in town."

"Don't some of your cousins' wives own the wedding dress boutique?"

"Yeah, but…" Galen studied the garment again, shaking his head. "Never mind. It's not important. What time are you on duty?"

"I'm watching the kids for the next two days. Then I have two days off. I'm planning to go check on my dad." Rose took a long look at the handsome man in her room, memorizing everything about him. "Did you need something, by the way?"

"Not really," Galen said. "I got stopped on the way to my room by the mention of you bidding on me. I'm sorry you were disappointed."

She raised a brow. "Did I say I was disappointed I didn't win you?"

He grinned. "Maybe I was the one who was disappointed." Then he kissed her, slowly and sweetly, and Rose felt her world shifting and changing. She leaned against him, curled her hands around his broad back and felt their bodies melt together.

A second later the storm that had been threatening all afternoon broke wide-open with a fierce thunderclap, blowing all the lights out without even a flicker. She gasped and stepped back from Galen.

Thankfully, it was pitch-black in the room, or he'd know just by looking at her face how much she wanted to toss that gown off her bed and drag him into it.

"Whoa," Galen said. "Where'd you go, beautiful? Don't leave a guy standing in the dark with empty arms."

"I'm looking for a flashlight."

"Don't do that. I know where my mouth is. I can lead you right to it."

His teasing finally coaxed away her nervousness. "Galen, don't you have a match?"

"I was hoping you wouldn't ask. Now that you have," he said, striking one and holding up the resulting flame, "I cannot by way of gentlemanly decree lie and say I do not have said match. But I liked what we were doing in the dark much better."

"Maybe your aunt is right about you." Rose groped in a drawer and found a flashlight, turning it on and setting it on the table with the beam upward. "Maybe you're not raffle material."

His laugh was low and sexy. "One thing you should know about my aunt is that she loves the theory of reverse psychology." He blew out the match and took the flashlight. "Follow me. We'll go make sure she has her flashlight. I worry about her and Burke falling."

"You're nothing if not a good nephew," Rose said, following him down the stairs. "Maybe it *was* reverse psychology. That would mean she thinks you are worth bidding on."

"Of course I'm worth bidding on. I'm the best catch at Rancho Diablo. Don't let my aunt fool you, cupcake. She's cast her line, and she's trying to reel you in. My advice is run while you still can."

Rose rolled her eyes behind Galen's broad back. "Why ever would I want to run from the best catch at Rancho Diablo?"

"Because," Galen said, "most ladies around here have found themselves with an empty hook."

"That's a shame," Rose said. "But then, I'm not really worried about the quality of my bait."

He laughed again, and she smiled, not worried at all.

"Jace," Galen said, once they were in the den. "Glad you're here. I'd like to call a family meeting tonight. We have a lot to discuss."

"Like the fact that you're planning to buy the ranch across the canyons?" Jace demanded. Rose heard the edge in his voice.

"Call the meeting if you have cell service," Galen said tersely, no longer laughing and happy the way he'd been a moment ago, and Rose knew that after tonight, everything at Rancho Diablo was going to change.

The storm had brought in dark clouds and knocked out the power. It felt as if a lot of energy had left, and anger and resentment had taken its place. A cold chill ran over Rose. She took the flashlight Galen handed her, and murmured that she was going to find Fiona.

But in the kitchen she found Running Bear, standing there silently, dark and tense. She stifled a shriek. "Hi, Running Bear."

He nodded.

"The guys are in the den, if you're looking for them."

He didn't move. "You went in the cave last night."

"Yes. I did."

"Come with me."

There could be no harm in going with Galen's grandfather. She followed him to the door.

"Not without me, Grandfather," Galen said from behind them.

"I knew you would come." Running Bear disappeared, and with a glance over her shoulder at Galen, Rose followed the chief.

"Where are we headed?" Galen asked.

"With Rose's permission, I would like to talk to her father. He knows much that may help us." Running Bear got into the jeep, waved a hand at Galen. "Drive, please." And with that, they took off into the storm.

Rose sat in the front with Galen, since Running Bear seemed content in the back. "Dad would love to talk to you. I'll let him know we're coming."

She dialed her father, relaying the information as Galen drove. "Dad says he's home, and to come on over. He'll enjoy having a visit from you." She glanced at Galen. "He specifically said 'the Callahans are welcome anytime.'"

"Good," Galen said. "Always good to know the welcome mat's out. So, Grandfather, why are we bothering Mr. Carstairs?"

"Sheriff Carstairs," Running Bear said. "Once upon a time, Sheriff Mack Carstairs was a Texas Ranger. That was a while ago, but he knows many people here in New Mexico."

"You're going to talk to Dad about the tunnels?" Rose asked.

"We need counsel," Running Bear said. "Government agencies are going to want to know that there are tunnels under our lands. We need advice on how to proceed before the government agents arrive."

"Dad has a lot of contacts still, Running Bear. He'll be happy to help." Rose looked out the window as the rain poured down. "He'll be pleased you're taking him into your confidence."

"Thank you," Running Bear said. "We need all the friends we can get now."

Rose glanced at Galen. His sidelong gaze met hers and she smiled at him. It seemed as if last night had happened forever ago.

And the kiss, even longer.

RETIRED SHERIFF MACK was a big man, bigger than Galen, who was no small fry himself. He was at least six-four in his boots, with long, shaggy white hair crowned by a worn straw Resistol cowboy hat. He enveloped his tiny daughter in a bear hug, and Galen saw at once that Rose was the apple of her father's eye.

He didn't blame the sheriff one bit for being very fond of his cute little apple.

"What you're coming to talk about, Chief," Mack said as he waved them to chairs, "is tricky business. The Feds are going to come in, make a mess of your property. It'll be on TV. The whole stew will have everybody in New Mexico up in arms, because they'll wonder where else tunnels are being dug." The big man tossed his hat on a sofa and grabbed a couple bottles of tea from the fridge. "Sorry. Don't have time to make my own."

"Dad," Rose said, "making tea doesn't take any time. You just like this sugary stuff."

"That I do." He grinned mischievously. "Now that you're gone and your sisters are married off, I can drink sugary stuff all I like."

"Dad!" she protested. "I'll brew up some real tea for you. Will you drink it?"

"I'll drink anything you make for me. It's hard not having her at home," Mack told Galen. "Hope you folks are taking good care of my little girl."

Galen was about to say, *Yes, indeed,* when Rose said, "Dad, I'm twenty-eight. No one needs to take care of me."

"That's what she always says." Mack grinned and looked back at Running Bear. "You could always try to flush them out, Chief. The problem is, they'll come back. And it's sort of skirting the law not to mention that they're there, you see. Smugglers and mercenaries and the like bring trouble, not just to your property, but surrounding ranches. Crime goes up. Soon you've got bigger problems on your hands."

Galen and Rose glanced at each other. She could tell he was giving her father's words his complete attention. Mack respected Running Bear and Galen. Maybe the four of them could figure out a solution.

"And it's dangerous for your kids," her dad added. "I've heard you're growing quite the brood out at Rancho Diablo."

Galen nodded. "Most of my brothers are happily married."

"Might seriously consider moving the kids," Mack

said. "I would, if it was my Rosebud." He glanced at her apologetically. "Mind you, I realize you doing so would put my little girl out of employment. But you might consider sending the kids and wives off to join their cousins. I know you've got a place in Tempest, too."

Her father leaned back, took a big drink of his sugary tea. "Now I've got myself in hot water with Rose. But I'm an honest man, Galen. You've got to figure matters will probably get uglier from here."

Galen stood, and Running Bear rose with him.

"We will think on your words," the chief said. "Thank you for seeing us."

"Anytime. Pardon me while I embarrass my daughter." He enveloped Rose in one last bear hug. "You come home soon, if you want to. Don't let this big rascal cowboy keep you away from your ol' pop."

"Dad!" Rose kissed his cheek, then stepped away. "I'll be back in a few days with a hot meal. I don't think you're going to be the kind of man who takes up cooking in his spare time."

"Nope. Too many ladies around here seem to like sending casseroles my way. And occasionally, I have a barbecue for the boys. Don't worry about me, Rose. You just be careful out there. I expect you to take very good care of my girl," he told Galen, and she made an impatient sound and headed for the door.

If her father didn't pipe down with all the protective advice, Galen was going to turn skittish on her. Then she'd be like Ash, finally giving up on a ghost she'd been chasing for too long.

Rose had no plans to give up on her cowboy.

Chapter Six

Rose wasn't entirely surprised when she heard a knock on her door that night. In fact, she was prepared for Galen's visit.

To her shock, Somer and Jace walked in.

"Hi," Jace said. "Is this a bad time?"

He eyed the plate of gingerbread on her nightstand, along with two cups of tea.

"Not at all," Rose said coolly. "How can I help you?"

"Somer and I are going to take a drive. She's working tomorrow. We'll be back in time, but could you keep anybody from looking for her if it comes up?"

Rose glanced from Jace to Somer. "What's going on?"

"We're in the mood for a road trip," Somer said. "If anybody looks for me, I don't want them to know I'm gone. With Jace," she clarified.

"Oh. I see." She shrugged. "I can tell them you've gone to visit your uncle Storm."

"And I've gone to—" Jace began, stopping when Rose held up a hand.

"I only cover for ladies. Men have to do their own dirty work," she explained. "It's a girl thing."

"Fine." Jace nodded. "Thanks, Rose."

"No problem." She studied the pair, who looked suspiciously nervous. "You realize that Galen may dig a little deeper, no matter what I tell him, when he realizes both of you have disappeared."

"Can't you keep him busy?" Jace asked.

Rose gave him her best stink eye. "I will do no such thing," she said, her tone disapproving.

"It's not what you think," Somer said.

Rose said, "I don't care what you two are up to. Leave me out of the particulars of the road trip, please. I've got enough on my hands as it is."

Jace glanced toward the cups and gingerbread. "You snack like that every night?"

"So what if I do?" she asked.

"Just never knew a lady who needed two cups of tea. Might as well get a mug," Jace said. "Save yourself a dirty cup, right?"

Somer tugged at Jace, who was going on like a beagle after a buried bone. "Come on, cowboy."

"That's right," Rose said. "I don't tell your secret, and you don't ask about mine."

"Understood," Somer said, pulling Jace into the hall.

"Wait," he said. "I'm not through teasing her. That's the best part of life at the ranch. What would we do if we didn't give each other the business all the time? It's an art form with us."

"Not tonight, it's not," Rose heard Somer say as they went down the hall.

Rose got up to close the door. It was getting late, later than last night when Galen had visited. Maybe he wasn't coming tonight. She reached to turn off the lamp just as her door opened.

"Whew. I thought they'd never leave," Galen said,

stepping inside. "I heard Jace say you'd brought me my midnight snack, you sweet girl. Thanks a million."

She put her hands on her hips. "I didn't say this was for you."

"But you didn't say it wasn't." He sat down and helped himself to gingerbread and tea. "Where are the smiley faces?"

"The what?"

He waved at her legs. "Your smiley-face nightwear."

"These are fine." She glanced down at her pajamas. "You have a problem with ladybugs?"

"Love ladybugs." Galen looked pleased with himself. "Just thought the smiley faces suited you."

"I'll keep that in mind." She sat down next to him on the bed. "So what did you decide about your dilemma?"

"I don't know. We need another family meeting. My brothers and Ash will need to vote." He sighed, sipped the tea. "Half of them will vote for burning out the tunnels. They'll want to go all Armageddon on Wolf's men, and Fiona, my warrior aunt, will be right there with that plan. The other half will want to stay this side of the law. We *will* stay this side of the law. And I appreciate your father talking with us today. He called me later to let me know he's discussing the issue with some of his contacts. He thinks we're in for a tough time around here, once the word gets out." Galen looked at Rose, put his gingerbread down. "You know your father's right, don't you?"

Her heart sank. "I'm not leaving, if that's where you're going with the Daddy-knows-best chat."

She sipped her tea, then crawled up onto the bed, bumping him over so he couldn't hog all the space with his big frame.

It felt really good, sitting so close to him.

Galen slid down next to her, their shoulders together— just as they'd been last night.

"I don't want you to leave. But if that's what it takes to keep you safe, that's what we'll do."

"I'm fine, except I'm sad that the kids will have to go." She sighed, thinking about the four Callahan children she'd come to love. "Maybe Kendall and Sloan would allow me to go with them."

"To Hell's Colony? They probably would. Or they might decide to go to Tempest. That decision is up to them." Galen pulled her close to him, so she rested on his chest. Rose snuggled down, loving the feel of him. He was hard and strong beneath her, and he smelled sexy, like fresh-cut cedar.

If she'd ever had any doubt she was falling for him, it fled her mind now.

"This probably isn't a good time to tell you this," Galen said, "but I think I have a crush on you."

She looked up at him. "I'm open to that."

"Really?"

"Why do you think I have gingerbread in my room? To feed the mice?" She snuggled against his chest again. "I was hoping to catch a big strong cowboy."

He pulled her face up so that his lips met hers, and for the second time, they kissed—really kissed, not just a brush of skin. Excitement swept Rose, and she rolled onto her back as the kiss deepened.

It seemed as if they kissed for hours, unable to get enough of each other. She pressed close to Galen, loving how his hands cupped her hard against him.

They heard someone in the hall, and Rose froze. Galen pressed against her, kissing her neck, her lips, and then lower.

"Galen!" she whispered urgently. "Someone is out there!"

"It's all right. We're not inviting them in."

He unbuttoned her pajama top and kissed her breasts with the same attention he'd paid to her lips. Rose no longer cared if someone might walk in. She was lost in the moment, lost in Galen, so happy to be in his arms.

"Let's get you out of this," he said, pulling off her pajamas.

"And don't you be shy," Rose replied, tugging his shirt off and reaching eagerly for his jeans.

"No one can accuse me of being shy." He tossed his jeans to the floor and kissed her belly. His warm lips caressed and teased, and he took his time exploring her, so that by the time he had kissed her all over, and made love to her again and again, early morning light was peeking in the window.

"I've got to go," Galen said, getting up to dress. "Not that I want to. Nothing more I'd rather do than let you tempt me back into bed."

"And I would," Rose said, dragging the sheet with her as she climbed from the bed. "But duty calls."

He followed her into the bathroom, kissing her. "This cookies-and-tea thing could become a habit," Galen said.

"Just cookies and tea?" She lifted a brow, challenging him to admit that he hadn't come to her room solely for treats of the gastronomic variety.

"We'll see," Galen said. "'Bye, beautiful."

She walked him to the door, checked the hallway carefully then blew a kiss his way. His face lit up, and Rose watched him head down the stairs.

The most wonderful night of her life.

She went to shower and get ready for the day, floating on air.

"Have you seen Jace?" Galen asked Rose when she came down for breakfast. Fiona and Burke were busy cooking up eggs, toast and sausage links, and his brothers were all present and accounted for—except Jace.

She looked adorably confused. "I just came downstairs."

"I didn't know if you'd run across him upstairs." Galen shrugged. "He'll show up eventually. Breakfast is his favorite meal of the day."

"I like it, too. Good morning, Fiona. Burke."

"Meeting tonight," Galen said. He had to work hard not to watch every move Rose made. It was hard to believe he'd spent the last several hours making love to her. He could easily skip breakfast, carry her back upstairs and do it all over again.

His brothers mumbled and murmured about a meeting being called, but his focus was pretty much on Rose. She was wearing yoga-style black stretch pants and a black top. Clearly, she was on her way over to watch the kids, and he adored her looking all sexy nanny.

Who am I kidding? She'd be sexy in a pair of jeans and an apron, working at the Books'n'Bingo Society, baking cookies.

I really love looking at her.

She made his heart happy. There was no two ways around that. Which scared him a little, because he didn't have a whole lot of room in his life for an emotional attachment right now.

On the other hand, he could make room for a woman as sweet as Rose.

"What are you mooning at, Galen?" Dante asked, and he jumped.

Tighe said, "You look like you've got indigestion or your jeans are too tight."

Everyone turned to stare at him. Galen sighed, tore his gaze away from Rose reluctantly. "I'm fine. Thanks for the concern, but I've never been better."

Of course, his gaze bounced right over to Rose when he said he'd never been better, and that was a dead giveaway.

"Oh-h-h," his brothers all said, and then Ash had to pipe in, too, and everyone glanced at Rose, who wasn't paying attention to any of them. She held a biscuit she'd slathered with Fiona's delicious strawberry jam, and was biting into it. Her blond hair was up in a high ponytail, and as Galen watched every move she made with her sweet lips, lust hit him so fast and hot his legs felt weak.

His brothers and sister gazed at him, their faces knowing. They were dying to tease him, give him jazz about falling exactly the way he'd said he never would: for an employee of the ranch. But beyond that, tumbling hard, like a boulder down a hill.

"Smooth, bro," Sloan said.

"This is not going to be pretty," Ash said, smirking at her brother. "You realize you're playing far out of your league."

Rose looked at them curiously, but then struck up a conversation with Fiona, totally oblivious to the deep hole Galen had just dug for himself. Now that his siblings had figured out that his heart was leaning in a certain direction, he was going to hear about it endlessly.

Galen sighed. "I might be playing far out of my league, but at least I'm in the game," he said crossly to his sister.

His family roared with laughter. "Meeting tonight," he reminded them. "Don't be late. It's important. And someone get word to Jace, wherever he's staged his disappearing act. One of you knows where Houdini Callahan is."

Then he retreated to the office to do paperwork, and think about Rose.

GALEN HAD EXPECTED that the meeting wouldn't go well. The topic was doomed to be met with tense questions.

What he hadn't expected when he told his family he was going to buy the ranch from Storm, in his own name, and that Fiona's raffle was off, was nods of acceptance.

"Sounds like a good idea to me," Sloan said. "If you need cash, I don't mind putting up a stake."

"I'd go in," Tighe said. "I'd back my brother in a heartbeat."

Falcon nodded. "Can't think of any one of us who deserves that ranch more than you, bro."

"True," Jace said. "After thinking about it, I decided that you raised us, sacrificed a lot. You'd do the most good for the land."

"As long as you name it Sister Wind Ranch, I'm all for it," Ash said, her smile mischievous. "You know it's a catchy name, and if you're going to start a dude ranch, that would look good on brochures."

Dante sat up. "A dude ranch! That's a great idea, brother!" He slapped Galen on the back.

"Who said anything about a dude ranch?" Galen

couldn't believe how boneheaded his family was. "Can you see me running a dude ranch?"

"What else would you do with that land?" Ash asked solemnly. "You're a doctor. Dr. Dude Ranch. It's not like you'd want to be a rancher, Galen. Or raise chickens or grow crops. What would you grow over there?"

He shook his head. "Look. I don't know exactly what I'll do with it. Well, I do know, actually, but running a dude ranch isn't in the plans." Galen was almost insulted that his siblings didn't think he had a plan.

"You do what you like," Jace said. "But you're no spring chicken, I might remind you. Cattle ranching's not for old guys."

Galen set his jaw. "You guys are numbskulls. The first thing I'm going to do with that land across the canyons is let the Feds run all over it. So get ready."

"Wow," Ash said. "You sure are slow about telling this story. What's going on?"

"It's what's going under," Galen said, and proceeded to tell them what he and Jace and Rose had discovered under the ranch across the canyons, and what he suspected might be underneath Rancho Diablo.

"Simple fix," Ash said. "We burn them out. Then fill in the tunnels with concrete."

Galen quickly held up a hand to restrain his hotheaded sister. "No burning anybody out. We're letting the law handle this."

Falcon looked displeased. "Not that they did much for our parents. Being in witness protection is hardly a life."

"That's true," Dante said. "Are we all going to need witness protection one day?"

Galen sank back into the sofa, sipped his whiskey. "I hadn't thought of that angle."

"Exactly. That's why we hold these councils, because seven heads are better than one," Ash said. "I personally won't enjoy living my life in hiding."

"How are we any safer if we destroy the tunnels?" Galen asked.

"He's right," Tighe said. "We're not. We might get caught by Wolf's thugs before we set the first charge."

"What are the tunnels for?" Sloan asked. "Smuggling? Or are they planning to tunnel under Rancho Diablo to ambush us?"

"All of the above," Ash said. "We won't let it happen. We're going to search every inch of this ranch and make certain nothing's under it. We owe that to our cousins."

Galen nodded. "You're right. We said we'd keep this ranch safe. So far, we have. But Wolf outthought us, hitting us from underground like this."

"Send Rose back into the cave," Falcon said suddenly. "Or Ash. We need to plant some recording devices."

Galen shook his head. "No one is going back in that cave. We shouldn't have put Rose down there in the first place. Jace and I didn't entirely realize what it was." They'd had no idea of what they'd discovered. And he'd had no idea Rose would be so thorough in her recon efforts.

He really admired her bravery.

"Where'd you go today?" he suddenly demanded of Jace. "You disappeared for hours."

"I was running errands," his brother replied.

"All day?" Galen frowned. "Weren't you scheduled for patrol?"

"I swapped with Sloan, no worries," Jace said, but Galen thought his brother looked a little too eager to end the conversation.

Still, he supposed it was none of his business.

"I'm glad none of you are angry about me buying the land. The idea was Running Bear's, so I hope it's a good one. Storm must have learned that something was going on with Wolf and his henchmen, because he was pretty eager to sell. We're not paying top dollar by any means."

"We'll all be happy to pitch in pennies," Tighe said.

"I still don't know if I trust the man," Galen admitted, "but I suppose since we're hiring his kin all over the place, I'll have to get over it."

"True," Ash said cheerfully. "Especially since Jace has got an epic thing going for Sawyer."

Jace turned a bit red. "Did I say that?"

"No," his sister said, delighted to be able to yank his chain. "Her cousin, Somer, did. By the way, I heard Somer had her eye on you at one time, Galen."

He started. "I don't think so."

"Apparently, she did. But," Ash continued in merry fashion, "she quickly figured out your interests lay elsewhere. She's now dating Dr. Brody, the vet in town." Ash looked at Galen with glee. "We're all betting the other interest is Rose."

"Don't bet," he said. "It's a dumb thing to do with hard-earned cash."

The siblings rose, signaling an end to the meeting. Ash grinned at him.

"I know you're not going to open a dude ranch, Galen. I was just giving you a roast."

"Thanks. I always need a good needling from my sister." He ruffled Ash's pale hair, which had now grown to her shoulders, and thought what a shame it was that Xav had tossed away the best girl on the planet.

Best girl besides Rose.

"What are you going to do about Rose?" Ash asked. "All the babies and children are going to have to leave, obviously, if you're fixing to swarm this place with Feds. So nannies aren't necessary here. And she's not a body-guard or sniper type of girl. Probably has never fired a gun."

"I suspect you're wrong about that." He figured Mack Carstairs was likely the kind of man who'd take his daughter hunting with him. And his grandchildren.

Galen's breath caught at the thought of grandchildren. "Holy smokes," he muttered.

"What?" Rose said. "What is it?"

He'd just spent a glorious night making love to Rose every which way from Sunday. If he was lucky, he might do it again tonight. What if he ended up like his bucket-headed brothers? Pregnant and no ring?

Rose wasn't the kind of woman to jump into a mar-riage just because she was expecting a child. They'd used a condom. Everything was probably fine.

He glanced over at Sloan, Tighe, Falcon and Dante, who were huddled in a corner discussing the tunnel problem. Dissecting it from every angle. Not thinking about women, because they had theirs.

Galen didn't have the one he wanted. And Rose wouldn't be an easy catch. She wouldn't want to go home and tell her big, tough-minded father that she was ex-pecting a child out of wedlock.

"You look like a ghost has infested our ancestors' graves," Ash said. "What's wrong, Galen?"

"I—" he began, but sudden thunder boomed out-side, pounding and rhythmic. He and his siblings gazed out the many windows. "Look," he murmured, though there was no need. The Diablo mustangs were galloping through the canyons, a dark, twisting ribbon.

"Legend has it they're a mystical portent of things to come," his sister murmured.

Galen felt a shiver touch him—not a ghost, but a stern premonition from out of nowhere.

"It's the Diablos," he said, suddenly hit by blinding clarity. "Wolf's tunneling under the canyons because they intend to destroy the Diablos."

The heart and soul and very spirit of Rancho Diablo.

Chapter Seven

When Galen didn't show up that night to share a midnight snack, Rose went looking for him. She tapped softly on his bedroom door, glancing around to make certain no one saw her there.

Galen opened it, glanced up and down the hall, then directly at her. "Nice pj's. I like the satiny look. Elegant." He dragged her inside and closed the door.

"What are you doing?" she asked, looking at the model of Rancho Diablo he'd built on a table in his room.

"I'm trying to prove my hypothesis," Galen said. "I think Wolf and his men built those tunnels because they're after the Diablos."

"Why?" She studied the very detailed map. "I thought the point was to get to Rancho Diablo and wreak havoc from underneath. And probably above, eventually. All it would take would be a helicopter or two, or a few cameras fitted on the oil derricks."

He stopped what he was doing and stared at her. "That's an angle I hadn't considered."

"Good." She looked at the model again. "So back to the Diablos."

"Those mustangs are the lifeblood of Rancho Diablo. This may be hard to explain," Galen said, "but we believe in spirits. We believe in our ancestors. This ranch was foretold in a dream to Jeremiah Callahan, who built it and this house we're currently living in."

It was a fabulous mansion, with seven chimneys, and done in the Tudor style. Rose had fallen in love with it at first glance, as did everyone else. Jeremiah and Molly Callahan had put every ounce of love and hope into the home, and then started their family here.

Only to have to give it all up, just like Galen's parents had.

Rose resolved to help Galen if she could. "How would Wolf destroy the Diablos?"

"By destroying their habitat. The canyons are a spiritual place for the mustangs. They don't live anywhere else. They're safe there. No one can capture them. They stay free, like our ancestors believed man and everything under the sun should be."

She looked at Galen, admiring the long hair falling carelessly across his collar as he stared at the model, at his big shoulders, strong and sexy under his shirt. "Can Wolf be stopped?"

"We will find a way. Somehow." Galen looked up at her, wrapped an arm around her waist and pulled her against him, kissing her deeply until it felt as if her breath left her and became his.

"Hey," he said, "we're going to get married."

She couldn't have been more shocked if the ground had opened up beneath her feet. "We are?"

"Yes. As soon as possible. Tomorrow."

Rose moved away from his side, trying to take in what was the strangest proposal she'd ever heard. "Why?"

"Because I need to take care of you."

She blinked. "I'm taking care of myself just fine. But thank you for the offer. I guess."

He shook his head. "It's not an offer. It's a marriage proposal. I want you to marry me."

"I always heard Callahans were terribly hard to tie down. That they avoid the altar like the plague." She moved to the opposite side of the table, putting the model between them. "What's going through your head, Callahan?"

"That I don't want to end up like my brothers—running around in circles trying to win their woman. I want to be married now. I want it to be right."

"They're married. They're happy. What's wrong with how it happened?" Rose was puzzled. "Not that I want to turn down a marriage proposal, but I would like to understand what I'm turning down."

"You're turning me down?"

"I don't even know what you're asking, exactly," Rose said, exasperated.

"I'm asking you," Galen said, pulling her gently toward him, "to marry me, be my wife."

"We've only known each other a few days."

"But we're sharing midnight snacks. And a little more. It's the *little more* that convinces me I'm marrying you."

She looked at him. "Galen, I'm trying to understand the workings of your mind, but it's like looking at a maze. Are you saying that because we've slept together, we should automatically get married?"

He nodded. "I waited a long time for a woman like you. If you become pregnant, I don't want you running off. Women that get attached to my brothers tend to do that." He looked alarmed at that prospect. "You can call me crazy if you like. I think I'm being smart."

He kissed her again, and she sensed he really was convinced of his plans. She gently moved back a step, needing to clear her mind, which she couldn't do while he was kissing her breathless.

"I don't know what to say."

"Except for yes, there's nothing else I want to hear you say," Galen said, reaching for her again.

"I need to think about it. Probably you should make love to me while I think."

"Okay, *that* works just fine," he said, and proceeded to convince her.

THREE DAYS LATER, Galen had Rose in Santa Fe at a justice of the peace before she could change her mind. "I'm a big believer in striking while the iron is hot," he told Jace, who'd come to stand in as witness. "The branding iron," he finished with a proud grin.

"Not to be chauvinistic or anything," his brother said, slapping him on the back. "I never thought I'd see the day you'd hotfoot it to an altar."

"Me, neither." Galen glanced over at Rose, who stood nearby, talking to her father and Ash, who had been her witnesses of choice. Mack had beaten them to Santa Fe, dressed in a Western tux and boots. Ash came along to serve as Rose's maid of honor, even though there was no such requirement. She'd said she had really come along just to see Rose put the ball and chain on her big brother, and wouldn't miss that for the world.

His family could laugh all they liked. He wasn't nervous. Rose was meant to be his—even if she didn't seem one hundred percent convinced that this was how she wanted to be married. But when he'd told her that she ought to grab him while he was up for grabs, she had shaken her head and said, "Guess that's an offer I shouldn't refuse. Consider yourself grabbed."

He'd rewarded her with a kiss and more.

"Here we go," Jace said cheerfully. "Time to help my brother commit himself to a lifetime of misery. I mean, happiness and joy." He grinned, pleased to jab at Galen. "And may I never follow in your footsteps."

Galen ignored him and took Rose's hand to step up to the justice. She smiled at him a little shyly, and he thought he was the luckiest man in the world to win such a cute little darling girl. His brothers had done things all wrong. They were cart-before-the-horse kind of guys.

Me? My horse is always in front of the cart.

"CONGRATULATIONS," HIS BROTHERS SAID after they'd flung rice on them at the top of the drive upon their return. Fiona and Burke had birdseed in tiny paper cups for the children to throw, and everything was right in Galen's world as he brought his bride home this beautiful late May day.

"As I said, you weren't getting any younger," Sloan said. "It's a good thing you tied him down," he told his new sister-in-law, with a kiss on the cheek and a hug. "He needed it so badly."

Galen heard Rose laugh. "I hope so," she said.

"I heard him say 'I do' with my own ears," Ash announced. "It was surreal, but worth the drive." She hugged Rose. "And I got a new sister to help me keep you ruffians in line."

"As if you really needed any help with that," Rose said, sending Galen a wink.

He felt warm all over.

"Bride," he said, "can I see you alone for a moment?"

"Now?" Rose asked. "I think Fiona wants us to cut the cake." She glanced around at the friends who'd stopped by to welcome them, and the family members, especially the brothers, who were eyeing the wedding cake with interest. The kids stood nearby, transfixed by the sight of cake, a punch bowl with floating fruit in it and gifts overflowing on a nearby table. "We'll be alone tonight, you know, and you can tell me anything you want."

Galen nodded, gave a put-upon sigh. "I guess I'll have to wait," he said in a low voice only she could hear. "But I plan to make up for it later. You know I've arranged for a pup tent in the canyons for our honeymoon night, just the two of us under the stars, listening to the coyotes and the crickets."

"A pup tent?"

"Sure. We want to be close." He grinned at her. "A pup tent sounds romantic, don't you think?"

She giggled at his teasing, her eyes wide and happy as she looked at him, and Galen felt as if he was king of the world.

SIX WEEKS LATER, Galen knew for sure he was king of the world.

"I'm pregnant," Rose said.

Galen laughed out loud. "That's awesome!" He held in the window-shattering yell he wanted to let out, and hugged his bride instead. "Let's celebrate with another night in the pup tent."

"No, thank you. Did I mention we're having triplets?"

He stared, staggered. "Triplets?"

She nodded, and Galen shook his head in disbelief. "Are you sure?"

Rose smiled. "I'd been having symptoms that weren't usual for me. I was tired a lot, among other things. Went to the doctor, who thought she heard more than one heartbeat, and recommended an ultrasound. Three little dots that are supposedly the hearts convinced the doctor that we're starting a family in a big way."

Galen wrapped his arms around her, holding her close. "Talk about a woman who can keep a secret. We're going to have to make some changes in our routine, babe. I want you doing nothing but sitting around looking pretty."

She kissed him on the mouth. "Right. That's going to happen."

He could tell his wife was of no mind to listen to his opinion on her resting.

"I have to go help Fiona at the Books'n'Bingo Society tearoom. I promised to help her and her committee plan the Christmas ball for this year, of which you will no longer be a part. Will you miss being put up for auction?"

"Nah. You caught me fair and square." He kissed her on the lips, lingering, wishing it was bedtime already so he could celebrate their happy news in naked fashion. She went out the door, looking darling in light blue shorts and a white blouse, and Galen congratulated himself again on being smart enough to put the horse in the forward position, cart behind.

Still, he was stunned, rocked by Rose's news. Overjoyed. He'd been wise to avoid his brothers' path of pregnancy first, proposal second. "An intelligent man learns from others' mistakes," he told himself, still in congratulation mode as he walked out the front door.

Storm was getting out of his truck, and Galen walked forward to greet him. "This is a surprise, Cash."

"Callahan." Storm nodded at him. "We need to talk about the real estate transaction we agreed upon."

"Everything's being handled by our agents. What's to talk about?"

"Let me congratulate you first on your recent wedding."

Galen nodded. "Hope to be hearing about yours and Lu's soon enough."

Storm shifted, looked toward his property. "Callahan, I don't want to be in the middle of your family's misery, as I believe I've mentioned, although perhaps not with those exact words."

"We don't invite anyone into our misery, Storm. Doubt you'd be the first to get an invitation." Galen frowned. "What's up?"

"I got a visit last night from the sheriff. He wants to use my property as a staging area. Looks like you're fixing to bring in some extra manpower."

Galen's frown deepened. "I'll have to talk to the sheriff. He hasn't mentioned this to me. Probably looking to see how an operation might proceed."

"I'm well aware that there's nothing I can do if the Feds are getting involved, and I'll make my peace with that." The big rancher's face wore a heavy look of concern. "But it was the second visit that has me perturbed."

"Why don't you come in the house and tell me exactly what's going on." Galen led him inside, though they'd never invited Storm in before. With two of Storm's nieces employed by Rancho Diablo now, maybe it was time to extend the olive branch.

He sat on the leather sofa in the den, looking around

appreciatively at the Native American rugs and art. "Nice."

"Thanks. As you were saying—"

Fiona hurried in, a pink sun hat on her head, her hair slightly mussed. "Galen," she said. "Oh, hello, Storm," she added in the next breath, and then looked at her nephew with huge, worried eyes. "There's some strange men heading this way, and Burke doesn't like the look of—"

Sudden yells erupted outside. Loud shouting, and what sounded like thunder. Galen jumped up, rushed to a window. "Wolf's men, no doubt," he said, and raced out the door.

"You best stay inside, Miss Fiona," Storm said, looking out a window. "He should have taken a gun with him."

"Oh, he's armed," Fiona said, bringing a rifle out of the kitchen. "Don't you worry about that." She opened a window and pointed the barrel out. "If you'll excuse me, Storm, I'm going to keep my eye on our visitors."

"That's just the thing, Miss Fiona," Storm said. "I'm here for your protection."

He gently took the rifle from her. Fiona straightened, gave him her frostiest glare. "What are you saying?"

"I'm saying Wolf sent me here to keep an eye on you especially." He sighed. "I really didn't want to be a part of this."

She glared at him. "You just let my nephew walk into a planned ambush?"

He appeared downcast. "Fiona, I tried to warn Galen. I was about to—"

"Get out. Get out! Go on!" She flapped her hands at

him as if he was mentally incapable of understanding her words. "Get out before I do something you'll regret!"

He sighed. "Fiona, I have to stay!"

She looked through the window, seeing Galen surrounded. "Look, you traitor. I'm going to pick up the phone and I'm going to make a call. You're not going to stop me. This is your last chance to turn away from whatever you've been talked into." She poked a finger into his chest to emphasize her every word. "And then you're going to fire that rifle out that window and scatter that crowd, while your brain still has any concept of honor left in it."

She began dialing.

"Fiona, I can't let you—"

She slapped his hand when he reached for her cell phone. "Try that again and you'll draw back a nub." She looked at her phone curiously. "I don't have cell service."

Storm didn't seem surprised. Fiona put her phone back in her purse. "So what's the game?"

"I don't know. They didn't tell me anything. All I know is that they're prepared to burn this place to the ground if I don't do what they're asking."

"So you're protecting us?"

He sat down on the leather sofa, the gun across his lap, not even bothering to point it at her. Fiona didn't figure he would put up much of a fight if she decided to bolt for the door. His heart just didn't seem to be in it.

Sudden gunfire sent her running to the window. "That'll be my nephews," she said with satisfaction, "and my niece, no doubt, and probably Burke. You better pick the winning team, Storm. We Callahans fight to win."

"I know," he said. "Why do you think I agreed to keep you pinned down, Fiona? Your family doesn't really need your help." He sighed again, clearly hating every aspect of his role in the attack. "Try your phone once more. I thought the sheriff would be here by now."

"Still dead. They've done something to the signals." She stared him down. "Galen and the others will run them off. You and I will be on bad terms for a long time."

"I know."

"You okay, Fiona?" Rose asked, walking into the den and stopping at the sight of Storm with a gun across his lap. "What's going on?"

"Not much," Fiona snapped. "Go away, Rose."

"The guys are shooting…." She looked at Storm again. "Hand me that rifle."

"I can't," he replied.

"Fiona, is this man holding you hostage while those bandits out there try to take over the ranch?" She glanced out the window, satisfied that Galen had everything under control. But she wasn't one bit happy about the situation. "Give me the gun, Storm."

"If I give it to you, they might come in and say I wasn't doing my job. They'll want to know that I was armed, and intimidated Fiona properly."

"You don't know Fiona very well." Rose looked at her annoyed friend. "They're losing out there, Storm. Hand me the rifle and I'll beat you with it, and you can convince them that you did your job."

"Rose!" Fiona said. "You're pregnant!"

"That doesn't mean I can't shoot him." Rose glared at their neighbor. "And to think I actually like your niece! What do you think Somer will say when she finds out you're one of *them!*"

Storm hung his head. "I had to do it. They threatened

to burn the place down if I didn't corral the old lady. I was supposed to tie her up and put her—"

"Old lady?" Fiona glared. "Watch your words or I'll peg you with my boot!"

Rose grabbed the gun out of Storm's hands. "Shame on you! I don't care what your excuse is!"

"I'm sorry," he said. "This is exactly why I want to sell out to Galen. There are too many dark undercurrents around. I want to live my life quietly and raise donkeys or chickens. Something more peaceful than being stuck between you guys and them."

"Who is 'them,' exactly?" Rose asked. "You need to tell me everything you know, if you're sincere about being with us."

"I am with you. I warned you, didn't I? Thought I was doing the best thing by being here with Fiona. I was afraid of what would happen if someone else was assigned to corral her."

"You should be *very* afraid!" Fiona snapped. "I'll never be kidnapped again, I can promise you that." She went into the kitchen, grumbling under her breath.

"What do we need to do so you don't get in trouble with them?" Rose asked.

"Wolf's not going to believe that I couldn't handle one little old lady."

Rose smiled. "You're forgetting what Fiona did to Wolf's lair in Montana."

"True, but—" Storm's eyes rolled back in his head and he fell to the ground. Fiona stood behind him with a frying pan.

"Our double-agent neighbor will sleep like a baby now," she said with satisfaction. "He never heard me coming up behind him. I learned something from Running Bear, after all."

Rose stared with horror at the big man prone on the floor. "Fiona! What if you've killed him?"

"I barely tapped him. Goodness, the boys I raised in this place withstood a lot more than that." She bent down, grabbed his ankles. "Help me drag him down the stairs to the basement."

"The basement!" Rose shook her head. "No, Fiona, we can't drag him anywhere." She wasn't sure what to do with Galen's feisty little aunt. Fiona seemed to be working from her own script, and Rose wanted no part of dragging the injured man down the stairs. Galen wouldn't approve of that plan, she felt certain.

Right on cue, almost as if she'd conjured him, Galen appeared in the doorway, disheveled, a little ragged from fighting. He had a bruise on his cheek and his knuckles looked a bit worse for wear, and Rose thought he'd never looked more handsome.

She flew into his arms. He hugged her, kissed the top of her head.

"Your work or Fiona's?" he asked, glancing down at Storm.

"We did it together," Rose said, not wanting to get the older woman in trouble. She suspected by the twinkle in Galen's eyes that he wasn't fooled, particularly as Fiona still held the frying pan.

"All right." Galen bent down to check out the big man, who let out a small groan. "Storm?"

"Fiona, you might want to put that away," Rose said, pointing to the frying pan. "Before Storm wakes up and all chance of neighborly relations are lost forever. Not to mention Lu's not going to be too pleased if she discovers you beaned her man."

"Oh, right. Of course." Fiona looked down at Storm. "I have something to say to Wolf, anyway."

She headed to the front door. With a frantic glance at Galen, Rose followed her. "I'll cover your aunt. You take care of your neighbor, Galen."

"Hang on." He caught up with her in fast strides. "Storm can take care of himself."

They followed Fiona as she approached Wolf. His minions had disappeared, likely heading back to whatever hole they'd come from.

"You go back," Galen told Rose. "This is too dangerous."

She bristled. "Too dangerous for what?"

"For you." He stopped her in her tracks and took her hands in his. "I want my bride to take my children back inside, where it's safer."

"You may have noticed we weren't that much safer there, Galen," Rose pointed out hotly.

"Go," he said, and her ire spiked. She glanced toward Fiona, who by this time was berating Wolf, no doubt for all his past sins, including kidnapping her last year and setting her neighbor on her.

"Come on, Galen! She might get kidnapped again. That was Wolf's sole goal at one time, to pick off a Callahan woman. And Fiona's the big cheese."

He held her back. "Go home."

She caught her breath. Glared at him, to no avail. "All right." Turning around, she marched back to the house, her pride stung.

"Hi," Storm said, moving to a sitting position as she

walked into the den. "Whoa. Have I ever got a head-ache."

Rose sighed. "Let me see your eyes."

She knelt down to look in his eyes. Checked the lump Fiona's pan had left on his head. "Thank goodness you're tough."

"Yeah." Storm rubbed his head. "What happened?"

"You tell me."

"One second I was here on Wolf's orders—which I wanted no part of, but he threatened Fiona, and I figured I was better on the inside than one of his henchmen. And the next thing I knew I was waking up, staring at the ceiling." He gingerly felt his head. "Got any aspirin?"

"Let's get you up on this sofa. I'll fetch you a bag of frozen peas to put on that. And I may call the doctor to come out, just in case."

Storm allowed her to help him to the sofa. "I don't need to lie down. I'm fine." He brightened. "Of course, I'd be better if I could have some of Fiona's cookies, and maybe some sweet tea."

"Medicine of the gods. I'll be right back. Don't move." Still steaming at Galen, Rose went into the kitchen to put cookies on a dish and get a glass of tea. How dare Galen think he could order her around, tell her to go inside? "He and I are going to have serious words when he returns," she murmured.

The kitchen door opened and Fiona huffed in. "Where's Storm?"

"In there. Waiting for your return. Wants you to show him your technique with a frying pan," Rose said, teasing.

Fiona nodded. "I may be glad to show him again. Let

me talk to him first. If I'm still annoyed after our chat, he'll have a two-lump day."

Fiona took the cookies and tea Rose handed her for Storm, and went through to the den. The kitchen door opened again. Galen came inside, sweaty and looking pleased with himself. He shouldn't have been so handsome, but the sweat and dirt only highlighted the blue of his eyes and the strength in his face.

Rose glared at him. "Have everything settled to your satisfaction?"

He grinned. "It's a good day at Rancho Diablo when the Callahans send the bad guys packing."

She handed him a cold glass of tea. "I don't appreciate being ordered off."

"I understand." He kissed her on the lips, placed a hand on her stomach. "And I hope you'll understand when I tell you that it's time for you to join Mack in Tempest until the babies are born."

Chapter Eight

By Thanksgiving, Rose was certain she hadn't married a Callahan but a ghost. It had been weeks since she'd seen Galen. He called, he texted, but his visits were few and far between, and usually under cover of darkness.

It had been a long six months.

He said he didn't visit often because he didn't want to lead bad guys right to her and Mack's door. Galen had a lot of respect for her father, or he wouldn't trust sending her to his home—but at the same time, he felt it was best to keep the pressure off.

Yet the pressure was on. The news that they were expecting triplets had made Galen even more protective of her, and of their babies. Which he was convinced were all boys, naturally.

Galen had never really been the same since the attack at Rancho Diablo. When he did come to see her now, she'd waken to feel him sliding into her bed, wrapping his big arms around her.

Mack walked into the kitchen to turn on the coffeemaker. "What are you doing up at this hour, girl? You're supposed to be on bed rest."

She stared out the window at the wintry landscape. "I can't sleep." She didn't sleep much, between thinking about Galen all the time, worrying about him, and the babies changing positions.

"Coffee?"

"No, thanks. But some herbal tea would be nice." She didn't feel like drinking anything, but the tea would warm her fingers. Her heart couldn't be warmed. Rose stared at the drifting snow and glanced at the thermometer outside the window. It was eighteen degrees at 5:00 a.m. She pulled her wool shawl a bit tighter around her. "I think I've finally accepted that this is the new status of my marriage."

Mack came to stand beside her, handing her a steaming cup. "I did warn you that marrying a Callahan was no way to live a dull life, baby girl. And they've got a proper shitstorm going out there. I get word from Sheriff Cartwright, who relays messages to me from Galen. They're covered up with trouble."

"I know." She sipped her tea. "Doesn't make it any easier. I want to be with my husband."

"Go get back on the sofa," her father instructed. "Doesn't do any good, disobeying doctor's orders."

The babies felt like bowling balls inside her. She knew she should go relax. Still, she lingered one more second at the window, hungry for a glimpse of the outdoors.

"Galen was right to send you here, you know."

She didn't reply, knowing her dad's words were valid, and yet resenting them just the same.

"See that tree?" Mack asked.

She nodded.

"Last night there was a scout in it. Thought I wouldn't see him. I always see them." He chuckled softly.

Rose turned to face her father. "What do you mean, you always see them?"

"There's been someone watching us since about a week after you came. Galen warned me to be ready to leave if things got too hot here. So I watch our little friends as they come and go. I know a bit about being under surveillance."

Her throat went dry. "You never told me."

Mack shrugged. "No point. You need to rest, not fret. My only reason for telling you now is so that you'll trust Galen to do the right thing."

"I do trust Galen. I just worry. Nothing's going to change that." She went to lie down, and her father sat across from her in an old leather recliner. Now she knew why he kept his shotgun loaded and nearby at all times. He also wore a holster with a gun at his back, under his jacket. Rose glanced toward the window again. Big, wet flakes of snow drifted down, enveloping the small house in silence.

"Sometimes I want to scream, but it wouldn't do any good." She picked up a book of sudoku puzzles and began to work in it.

Mack chuckled and got up to start a blaze in the fireplace. "In a month, you'll have so many babies to take care of, you'll want to scream for another reason." He smiled. "You were a good baby. I'm sure yours will be just as good. I'm looking forward to being a grandfather. Since your mom's been gone, and then you left to work, it was too quiet around here." He zipped his vest and headed outside for more firewood, and Rose put the sudoku aside. She wasn't in the mood for games.

She'd brought danger here. Even the simple act of her father going outside to bring in more logs for the fire was something to be worried about. She knew that from the attack on Rancho Diablo—one moment all had been well on a sunny day, the next, all hell had broken loose.

When she'd asked Galen how they'd run off Wolf and his men, he hadn't said much. He didn't want her to worry. She'd resented him shutting her out, but she'd also understood.

He was concerned about her stress levels during her pregnancy, and wanted her to feel safe. Secure.

She felt anything but.

After he built up the fire, her father glanced at her again. "I'm going out for a bit to check on the cattle. Will you be all right? Can I get you anything?"

"I'm fine. Going back to sleep. Thanks, Dad." She snuggled down in the blanket, basking in the warmth from the fire. The babies wrestled in her stomach, fighting for space. Rose smiled with contentment, putting a hand over her tummy as she drifted off.

She awakened many hours later when Galen put a hand on her stomach. "Galen! What are you doing here?"

"I called your phone to say I was coming out. Tomorrow's Thanksgiving. I want to celebrate with my family." He kissed her on the lips, and Rose sighed with happiness.

"I'm so glad you're here."

"I know you are." He gave her a teasing wink. "Is there room on that sofa for Dad?"

"With the four of us?" She glanced at the armchair opposite. "Where's my father?"

Galen touched her hair, ran a finger down her cheek. "I didn't see him, but I came in the back door."

Rose sat up and looked at the fire, which had gone out. "Galen! He didn't come back!"

"Mack didn't come back from where?"

"From checking on the cattle! He got more firewood, then said he was going back out for a bit!"

Galen jumped to his feet. Panic swept over her.

"I'll find him. Don't worry."

"Be careful, Galen." Of course she was worried. But Rose didn't say that, because it wouldn't serve any purpose. Galen strode out, and the door slammed.

"Oh, no," she whispered to herself. A trembling started in her limbs. She put a hand over her stomach, willing herself to be calm, frustrated that she couldn't go help Galen find her father. The snow had continued falling throughout the day and was now much deeper, so her father's footprints would be long covered.

Rose got up with an effort and went to the window to stare out. "Still snowing," she murmured. She glanced toward the trees where Mack had said he'd seen the scout, gasping when she realized she hadn't told Galen they were being spied on.

A sudden memory of the attack at Rancho Diablo goaded her into action. She had to tell Galen he might be walking into danger. Rose grabbed her coat, and reached for her phone to text him. Scout on property.

She pulled on a pair of green rubber boots, then grabbed one of Mack's shotguns from the rack on the wall.

Shots erupted outside, and Rose gasped again. Pain sliced across her abdomen, doubling her over.

GALEN COULD SEE there was trouble the moment Rose's face had filled with fear. Mack had been gone too long. Galen had known in his heart of hearts that he should have moved Rose and Mack farther away, maybe all the way out to the compound in Hell's Colony. He'd been selfish, wanting her close by so he could visit her. But he'd left her in the path of danger.

It was damn cold outside. Galen headed to the barn, hoping that maybe Mack had gotten distracted with some work with the horses.

That's not what had happened. Mack would never leave his baby girl alone for very long, especially not this late in her pregnancy, when she could go into labor at any time. With triplets, who knew?

Galen had left her here because he'd known Mack was strong, could take care of himself and his little girl. But when he saw Mack facedown on the floor in the barn, he realized he should have sent more than one reinforcement.

The doctor in him went into instant medical mode. He charged toward his father-in-law without another thought.

All hell broke loose. He heard a bullet scream by his head, so he jumped toward Mack, dragging him into a stall. Checked his pulse—it was strong, steady—and noted that the older man was out cold and his extremities were chilled. He'd been lying there awhile.

Galen grabbed his mobile, hit one button that would send out the call he needed.

"Hello?" Ash said.

"Mack's down. We're under attack."

"Hang on."

Galen checked Mack's breathing, which was clear and regular. The man was still unconscious, and there was nothing he could do but wait. Bullets flew outside—there was more than one shooter, so the bodyguard he'd put on the place was doing their job—but there was no telling how long he and Mack would be safe. Galen held the sheriff against him, wishing he had a gun, or even one of Jace's "party favor" explosives.

But he didn't. He wasn't like his brothers, who were better trained in military technique and survival. He was the thinker in the family—his focus was on curing the sick. "Damn it," he muttered, and Mack opened his eyes.

"Galen... What the hell?" Rose's dad struggled to get to his feet, but Galen pulled him back, trying to keep the sheriff warm.

"Stay still. We're under fire."

Mack stiffened, pulled away. "I've had my eye on that son of a gun for weeks. Did he get me?"

"I guess so. Stay still. He knows we're in here, but the guard I put on this place is doing her job."

"Guard?" Mack looked at him.

"Bodyguard. Figured you could use one or two around here."

Mack grunted. "Could have told me."

"Could have, but I needed you to stay sharp, not rely on a new hire. Frankly, I wasn't all that certain about this bodyguard. It was the best I could do on short notice. As time went on, I realized she was doing a good job."

"She?" Mack's brows beetled. "You can explain that later. Where's Rose?"

"In the house, keeping her head down, I hope." His gut clenched at the very thought of her getting near a window. She'd make a sweet target for Wolf's thugs. "Give me your hunting knife, Mack. Your holster's empty, so they obviously took your gun."

"I'm not giving you anything if you're going to go off in a hotheaded hero attempt." Mack frowned. "I've got a helluva headache, by the way."

"No doubt a minor concussion. There's a bit of blood.

I'm thinking you got beaned pretty good. Hand over the knife you keep in your boot."

Mack passed it to him. "I'm calling my daughter."

"Good idea. Tell her to lock herself in a bedroom and stay the hell away from windows." Galen crawled toward the stall door, heard another shot pop off and decided not to risk it at the moment. "They've got decent-size magazines. I'd say eighteen rounds. I've counted that many shots, at least. We might be here awhile, but I've got backup on the way."

"I warned my daughter about marrying a Callahan," Mack said. "Rose, baby. Pick up."

He looked at Galen. "She doesn't answer."

Galen's blood went thick and cold in that instant. Every fear he'd guarded against, tried to protect himself against, slammed into him, suffocating him and searing him with tight ties to the past. He'd felt these emotions before, when his siblings had been young, when their parents had gone away. Suddenly, he'd been responsible for raising people he hadn't thought much about in his quest for a medical degree. Life in the tribe taught you independence, yet it also taught deep faith and community.

Just like that, he'd become head of a household, a family that was in danger. He'd had to think fast, make decisions on behalf of his siblings, acting in a way that benefited the whole. And all the while, be very afraid that they'd never see their parents again. Running Bear had guided him, but at the end of the day it was Galen's duty to lie awake at night, washed in new fears that perhaps he wasn't the right one to lead them all. "I'm going to find Rose. Will you be all right here? I expect backup any second."

Mack nodded. "Normally I'd tell you not to be a hero, or a dumb son of a gun, as the case may be, but I'm scared to death for my daughter. If you go left out of the barn, you'll be only a few hundred yards from the house. Run like hell, not in a straight line, and hit the back door. I left it unlocked because I was only stepping out to check on the cattle. Didn't expect to be gone more than five minutes."

"Got it." Galen stuck the six-inch blade in his belt and crouched at the stall door.

"I'm going to count to fifteen from the moment you leave this stall. Then I'm running out the opposite way, to draw the fire. Make sure you don't get picked off in the last five feet to the house, because that's where you'll be a sitting duck."

Galen tensed. "I don't need help. You stay right here. Rose'll kill me if anything happens to you."

"Nope. Not gonna do it. And since you won't be here, you have no say in it, son." Mack nodded. "That's the hand you're playing with at the moment, so get a move on and find my daughter. My ticker's acting up at the thought that she might have been taken like your other Callahan women."

"Damn it." The same thought had occurred to Galen but he'd pushed it away. She'd never survive what Fiona had been through, or Taylor, or— "Count fast. I'm a good runner."

"Not in fresh, deep snow and boots, you're not."

"Try me." He might have been a nerd in school and in the family, but he was fast. "See you on the other side."

Galen slipped from the stall when the shooting went silent. Most likely this was his best chance; they were probably reloading. Maybe his dash from the barn wouldn't be noted fast enough.

Maybe it didn't matter.

He had to get to Rose.

Chapter Nine

Galen sprinted like he never had before and dived through the back door, just as Mack had advised. Not a shot had been fired. In fact, it was deadly silent. He caught his breath and realized why it was so quiet.

His family had arrived. Ash would have notified any Callahan cousins who were currently staying at Dark Diablo, the Callahan ranch in Tempest. Ash was probably on her way herself, or Jace. Someone had gotten to the shooter, or maybe the bodyguard Galen had hired had taken him out.

He'd let the family handle it. Staying away from windows, leaving the lights off, he strode quietly into the den.

His heart fell into his stomach when he saw Rose on the couch, clearly in pain. "Babe! What's going on?"

"Galen!" She gasped. "I heard the gunfire! Where's my father?"

"He's fine. What's going on with you?"

He knew what was going on by looking at the placement of her hand on her stomach and the sweat on her face.

His wife was in labor.

"Why are you wearing boots?"

"So you can take me to the hospital," she said, closing her eyes. "I don't think the babies enjoyed all the excitement."

He stroked her brow. Could he get his wife out of here without drawing fire? It was silent as a tomb outside; he'd just have to assume the shooter was dead.

Galen could call an ambulance. But Rose needed to get to Santa Fe, where her doctor who specialized in multiple births was located.

She groaned, and the sound was full of held-back pain. Rose wasn't going to make it to Santa Fe.

"Let me help you up." Outside, he saw flashing lights, which meant that squad cars had arrived. Tempest's finest were on the scene to protect their sheriff and his family.

"I'm not going anywhere without Dad. I can't leave him out there, Galen."

"I promise you he's safe. The cops are here, my family's here. The shooter's probably dead by now. I've got to get you to the hospital before we have babies right here in the den."

"You're a doctor. You could handle it."

He felt a shiver cross his skin. "Not delivering three babies, beautiful. Obstetrics is not my forte. Let me help you up."

He carried her, with one ear tuned to the sounds outside. A police cruiser was parked beside his truck, so Galen felt he had a good chance to get her away safely. "It's all over, baby girl. Hang on. By tomorrow, we'll be parents."

"My father," she said in a weak voice.

"Everything's going to be fine. Try not to worry. Think about those three little babies. Remember when you said you didn't want to know what we were going to have? I have a feeling we're about to find out just in time to put their names on their Christmas stockings." Galen put the seat belt around her and closed the door, telling himself that this wasn't going to be their life together.

History wasn't going to repeat itself. He wasn't going to live on the run the way his parents had—he'd fight for the sake of his three unborn children.

TEN HOURS AND an emergency C-section later, Galen stood in the presence of three tiny baby boys, so small he figured he'd seen bigger baked potatoes. That was an exaggeration, but their small size alarmed him. They didn't look like children who might grow into bull riders or military personnel.

They looked small and fragile, and his heart broke.

Ash came to stand beside him to peer through the nursery window of the neonatal ICU. "Hard for me to believe you're actually a dad, big brother."

"Me, too. Hard to believe those are my sons."

"They look healthy," she said cheerfully. "They'll grow, although it may not seem like it today."

"Thanks." Galen didn't feel any better. It was his fault his sons were born early, and now lay with tubes sticking out of them and monitors attached to every conceivable body part that could be monitored.

He wanted to make them strong and big—and he couldn't. "That littlest one, the one no bigger than my thumb…" he said, exaggerating because he was ill with fear. "The doctor says we'll know in twenty-four hours if he can pull through."

"Oh, Galen." Ash rubbed his back. "Everything's

going to be fine. He's a Callahan. He'll grow up to kick butt."

Galen's chest tightened with fear. Maybe, maybe not. He wasn't certain he picked up a lot of life force in that tiny little body. It seemed a bad sign that everything was being fed into his sons with tubes.

A series of bad decisions he'd made had led to his three sons being born too soon, and maybe too weak, to survive. It was his fault, and he knew it in his soul.

"How's Rose?" Ash asked, laying her head against his shoulder.

"Brave as always. Braver than me." He grimaced. "Where's the sheriff?"

"Mack? He's resting at home. Feels fine, except for the bump on his head and his pride being a bit dented." Ash smiled. "Rose gets all that toughness from her father."

He'd relied on that toughness to keep his family safe. "I blew it, Ash."

She rubbed his arm and kept her head against his shoulder, supporting him. "You couldn't have changed what happened if you'd been there, Galen."

"I should have warned Mack." Actually, he should have been there with his wife and kids, every minute. He'd known that. "I wanted to be at Rancho Diablo in case something big happened. Thought I could be both places at once." He sighed. "And maybe in my heart I didn't think the worst threat would follow Rose to Tempest."

He left his sister and his babies with a sad glance and went into his wife's hospital room. Rose looked at him with a tired, happy face.

"Are they beautiful?" she asked.

He kissed her forehead. "So beautiful they break my heart a little."

"You're sweet." She smiled at him fondly. "Dad just called. He says he'll be here in a while."

Guilt swamped Galen. "I don't suppose we could convince him to rest."

"You can try, but you'll get an earful." Rose pointed to the gallery of bouquets and balloons that filled her room. "See those flowers? Those are from your cousins."

He didn't, couldn't care. "There's something I have to tell you."

"Sit here on the bed with me." She patted the space beside her. "Get it off your chest."

"I don't think I hired the best help."

"You mean the scout?" Rose shrugged. "Good enough to run the shooter off, or get him. Anyway, Dad knew someone was watching us. He had an eye on him all along."

"The scout was Somer." Galen knew they'd been outplayed.

Rose blinked. "You think it was Somer who attacked my father? We were attacked by someone hired to guard us?"

"Looks that way."

"No. Somer is Sawyer's cousin. She wouldn't do that." Rose shook her head. "I don't believe it. The sheriff is wrong."

Galen didn't think so. "I knew there was something off about her the first time I met her. Her aura was dark. I felt darkness when we talked. I should have heeded my instincts."

Rose put a hand over his. "It doesn't matter. If you're right, and Somer was sent by Wolf to scare us—or worse—then Sheriff Cartwright in Diablo will see she's put in jail. I don't believe it, myself."

It had been a kick to the gut when he'd found out his family had captured Somer.

"Anyway, what was the point?" Rose asked. "It wasn't like I could have gone anywhere. I wasn't really a target, was I?"

"I don't know." Galen had wondered the same thing. "It would have been obvious to anyone that you couldn't travel. Perhaps they were just trying to rattle our cage, let us know they have spies everywhere."

"My poor father." Rose shook her head. Then her expression turned serious.

"I didn't realize you'd hired someone to protect us. Dad didn't know, either." She looked at him, her gaze suddenly perplexed. "Who was covering us, Galen?"

He sighed, wishing he didn't have to say. Felt a little foolish, considering what had happened. No, he felt really dumb, as if he hadn't paid attention to the warnings he'd felt inside him all along.

He looked at his wife, wishing he'd been wiser. It was too late for regrets now. "Sawyer Cash," Galen said.

A WEEK LATER, Rose was allowed to go home. She took one baby with her—little Ross Galen, who was stronger than his brothers. The other two were still tiny, but flourishing, though Riley Galen wasn't quite as hardy as his brother, Mack Galen. She'd given all three boys middle names after their father, because as far as she was concerned, Galen was the finest man she'd ever known, besides her own dad. If all three of her sons could grow up anything like him, she'd consider herself a mother who'd done her job.

But no matter how much she loved Galen, Rose had to admit that something had changed between them, and it wasn't just the babies' arrival. Galen stayed with her at night, helped her with Ross, but he was distant. Almost as if he had a lot on his mind and didn't want to share it.

Then again, it could be her imagination. Rose knew she was probably hormonal and tired. She put it out of her mind and concentrated on little Ross.

Galen brought her in some soup. "Hey, beautiful."

Rose smiled. "Hello, handsome."

"Your father's gone out for a bit. Think he and Sheriff Cartwright are in cahoots over something." Galen sat down next to her. "Your father doesn't share a whole lot of details."

"He's trying to get Somer off," Rose said, feeling cranky about the whole thing. "He doesn't want charges pressed."

Galen raised a brow. "Why? She gave him a minor concussion."

"Dad said it was barely a tap, and that you Callahans were bound to drive anyone nuts. That Somer was just doing her job, and besides which, he thinks he was attacked by a man. He thinks she's being framed."

Galen sank back into the chair across from her bed, glanced over at Ross in his white bassinet. They had three ready, one for each baby when they were finally allowed home. Rose was hoping for Christmas, but she was pretty certain that would take a miracle.

"Framed?" Galen repeated. He looked stunned.

"I don't really want to talk about it," Rose said. "I like Somer. At least I did—or still do—until we know exactly what happened that night. So I'm not getting involved. I'm going to sit here and do nothing but enjoy being a new mother."

She couldn't look at Galen. It was true what her father had said in the beginning, that with Callahans there came a lot of drama and agony. He'd warned her. Galen was worth it, of course—she loved him—but she had three sons to think of now. They might be a part of the Callahan legacy, but that didn't mean she was going to allow them to be part of the sacrifice that went along with being part of that legendary family.

Chapter Ten

"Fiona's here," Galen told Rose the next morning. "Do you feel like company?"

Rose nodded. "I'd love to see her. Can you hand me something to wear?" Even though she was sore, she didn't want to been seen in the oversize T-shirt she had on.

"I've always been partial to this *Dark Shadows* T-shirt you were wearing the night we sent you down into the cave." He grinned, and she caught a flash of the wild-eyed man she'd fallen in love with. "I don't suppose that's what you want, though."

"Something with buttons. I don't want to pull any stitches. I'm still moving pretty slow."

He nodded and left the room for a moment, returning with a white box with a big pink bow on it, which he gave her with a wink. "Maybe this will fit."

She shook the box. "Magic wedding dress? Do I finally get my turn?"

He seemed thunderstruck. Rose laughed. "Don't look so scared."

"I'm not scared. I'm surprised." He sank onto the bed, smoothed a strand of hair behind her ear. "You never said you wanted to be married in the magic wedding dress."

"I heard that a woman hasn't really caught her Callahan until he's seen her in the Callahan dress of dreams."

"You've caught me," Galen said, kissing her hand. "Oh, you've caught me. And I like it."

"That's what I want to hear."

They gazed at each other, and just for a moment, Rose thought she could feel the sparks of affection they'd shared before. She wanted to feel those sparks—wanted her husband to be in love with her.

"Well, go on. Open it," Galen said. "If you don't hurry, Fiona will probably come busting in here to hold the baby."

Rose undid the box, lifting out a beautiful white nightgown and robe with tiny pink roses in lovely lace scattered down one side. "I've never seen anything so pretty. Thank you, Galen." She leaned over and kissed him on the lips, seeming to surprise him.

"Well, the saleswoman assured me it would be easy to wear after a C-section," he said gruffly. "I personally like you naked the best, but I realize social conventions must be observed."

"Yes, they do." Rose slipped on the gown, buttoning the front. "I feel like a princess."

"That's because you are." He helped her into the matching robe, and smiled. "I get to take it all off of you later, and that's the part that makes me happy. Enjoy your visit."

He called for Fiona as he left the room, and it was like a whirlwind of pink swept in, instantly chasing off the gloom Rose had been feeling lately. "Fiona!"

"The cavalry has arrived!" Fiona exclaimed, kissing her on the cheek and then spying the baby in his bassinet. "Don't you worry, handsome. Aunt Fiona's here to take care of you. And I know a thing or two about what little boys like." She ran a slow, gentle palm over Ross's back and grinned at her most recent niece-in-law. "Looks just like Galen. A little prune-faced and puckery around the mouth, but otherwise human."

Rose giggled. "You wouldn't be secretly bragging about your movie-star-handsome nephew, would you?"

Fiona sat down in the chair across from the bed, settling herself in and setting the basket she'd carried with her on the floor. "Bragging's unseemly, my girl. Luckily, in our family we just tell the truth, and that seems to be good enough. Galen's handsome, if you like them tall and rangy and eggheaded."

Rose laughed. "Oh, don't make me laugh, Fiona."

"Laughter is what cures the soul. Now," she said, leaning forward, "tell me everything."

"Everything about what?" Rose looked at the Callahan matriarch. "Is there something I should know?"

"What happened the day the babies were born? You weren't expecting to have the babies that day, I know. The Christmas ball is next weekend, and as I recall you'd planned your C-section for after that. Galen said there was a furious hubbub out here, and you went into labor early."

"It's true. But I don't know as much as I should, I guess." Rose shook her head. "I try not to think about it. My dad's back to normal, and Galen's got this place loaded with bodyguards, so I just stay in my gentle cocoon of ignorance."

Fiona nodded. "A good thing indeed."

"There's so much I don't understand," Rose said. "Like why Sawyer Cash and her cousin Somer would be on opposite sides. Why Galen hired Sawyer if he doesn't really trust Somer and Storm Cash."

"You have to ask him," Fiona said, handing her a pink fabric bag that smelled like chocolate chip cookies.

Rose could feel her resolve melting. "I told myself no sweets after the babies were born, so I could get my figure back. I gained forty pounds! But I can't resist your cookies, Fiona. You're trying to get me off the subject."

"You can ask Galen those questions," Fiona said, making Rose hesitate as she reached for a cookie.

"No, I don't think I can."

"He'll tell you. You have a right to know," his aunt said gently.

Unease settled over Rose. She looked at Fiona. "He was trying to protect us."

"Of course he was." She pulled a knitted cap and booties from her basket. "Look at these. Turned out fine, if I do say so myself." She handed the booties and cap to Rose. "I've got a set for each baby," she said proudly.

"They're lovely," Rose murmured. "Stay on your point, please."

"Galen didn't know Somer was planted here by Storm. I think everything's gotten out of hand with our neighbor," Fiona said. "Wolf's got him by the…by the scruff of his neck, I think."

"I wouldn't be surprised."

"My guess is that Storm was trying to get his nieces out of there, both of them." Fiona leaned closer. "He told me that he was afraid they were in danger from Wolf, that Wolf had threatened to use his nieces as leverage if Storm didn't do what he was told. Storm's a big, tough man, but we knew he wasn't happy with his role in the attack on Rancho Diablo the day you and I were threatened."

"So Storm asked Galen to hire Sawyer? Then why would Somer have ended up on the bad side?" Rose stared at Fiona, her heart beginning to pound uncomfortably hard.

"Not exactly," Fiona said. "Galen hired Sawyer because she's been keeping in contact with Galen while she's staying away from Jace. Jace has annoyed her on some matter, and I'm not certain about all that at the moment. Anyway, only Galen knew where Sawyer had gone off to. He thought she did good work, that he could trust her with you, so he hired her. Good decision," Fiona said, nodding. "But then Storm sent Somer out here, as well."

Rose blinked. "But I've defended Somer to Galen. Told him I didn't think she would have harmed my father or me. I consider her a friend. We were the new girls at the ranch."

Fiona looked sympathetic. "Sometimes it's hard to know who our friends are. Galen knows this. He feels very guilty about not having this place locked down better."

"Why wouldn't he have told me?"

"My guess is Galen doesn't want you to know he was the reason you and your father were shot at. He knows your dad was hesitant about you working at Rancho Diablo in the first place, and that the sheriff warned you against falling for a Callahan." Fiona settled back in her chair. "Storm is beside himself that Somer shot at her cousin, Sawyer. That's how I know what I'm telling you is true."

Rose's heart seemed to shatter into a million pieces. "This is so hard to believe."

Fiona shrugged. "Stranger things have happened. Still, you need to talk this over with Galen. If my stubborn nephew isn't going to cough up the truth, you must make him. It's the only way you can make decisions."

"Decisions about what?" Rose asked, feeling sad and a little sick.

"There are many you must face," Fiona said. "You have three sons. They'll be raised to fight the Callahan fight. It's something you'll have to accept, Rose. There's no halfway mark on the race we run."

Rose thought about the cave she'd seen, and the painting of Running Bear. There were tunnels running under the canyons back of Rancho Diablo that were fortified, an underground city whose occupants might crush the Callahans if they weren't careful.

And now Fiona was telling her that her sons were part of that legacy. That her husband had hired a traitor as a bodyguard to protect her.

That her marriage might not be the stuff of dreams.

BY THE TIME FIONA LEFT that afternoon, the house had been transformed into a Christmas wonderland. Decorations and lights graced practically every corner, and a tree that looked as if it had been created for a Hollywood set glowed in the den near the fireplace. Galen doubted Mack had seen such a holiday extravaganza in his home in years.

If his wife was cheered by his aunt's elfish ministrations to the house, Galen wouldn't have known it from the look on Rose's face when he walked into the bedroom to help her feed and change baby Ross.

"Looks like Mrs. Claus was here," Galen said, kissing his wife and then his son. "How are you feeling?"

"Fine." She looked at him. "Fiona's energy has lifted me to the next level."

He grinned and sat next to her, taking the baby. "Think you're going to have Thing Number Two tomorrow, by the way. I just went to see the babies, and they're progressing nicely. They've got the nursing staff wrapped around their tiny fingers."

"Sort of the way you wrapped me around your finger." Rose sighed.

"That didn't sound like a lady who's happy," Galen said, kissing her again. "Did my aunt wear you out?"

"She brought up some things we should probably discuss."

"Uh-oh. That's the last time my aunt passes through that doorway."

"Can we be serious for a minute?"

"We can be serious for longer." He nuzzled her neck. "In fact, I look forward to being very serious with you in a couple of months, or whenever the doctor greenlights you, whichever comes first."

"Galen," Rose said, and he noted that she hadn't responded with her customary eagerness. "Did you hire Sawyer Cash to guard Dad's house?"

He nodded. "I did. She's a good bodyguard. She and Jace have gotten crosswise for some reason, and she wanted to get away for a while. I know that my brother could test the patience of a saint—"

"It's a Callahan thing."

"I don't debate that." He kissed her lightly on the lips. "However, she asked if I knew anyone who might need a bodyguard, and I said I wouldn't mind having someone out here keeping an eye on things. I thought it was a smart plan—until it wasn't."

"What went wrong?"

"I didn't anticipate Storm sending Somer out here. Of course, having two cousins shooting at each other is a recipe for disaster on so many levels it's scary." He shook his head. "I hired Sawyer just as easily as I would hire Ash. Never crossed my mind to look at the job differently because she's a woman. I knew Wolf would send a scout out here, but I didn't think he'd send someone with orders to shoot."

"It's horrible," Rose said. "Coincidence?"

"I believe so. Sheriff Cartwright has Somer in custody, and she certainly seems horrified she was shooting at her cousin. Somer claims she had no idea this was your house, either. That she thought she was *protecting* this house when she spied an intruder, which of course was no trespasser firing on her, but Sawyer," Galen said. "I'm not sure how much of that I buy, but Storm's her uncle. She wouldn't doubt his instructions. And if Wolf told Storm he needed someone on this house, he wouldn't have thought that his nieces would end up firing on each other—or you. I can tell you right now that Storm wouldn't let anyone fire on a Callahan. He may have gotten caught up on the wrong team, and I know he's frightened, but I believe in my heart that he wouldn't try to hurt a Callahan."

"Not if he knew what was good for him."

"Anyway," Galen said, "let's not worry about this. We don't have the full story, and I just want you thinking about healing and about little Ross. And we should celebrate that one of his brothers comes home tomorrow."

"All right. I think I'll go to sleep now."

It wasn't like his wife to be so withdrawn. Maybe she was tired…. Of course she was tired. Carrying triplets stressed the system, as did the C-section, from which she was still healing. Galen put a blanket over her lap and retreated to find Mack, hoping that if he left—and if baby Ross stayed quiet a bit longer—Rose might get some rest.

She'd sounded so worried, and he couldn't blame her. Any new mom would be scared of the situation Rose had found herself living in.

He had moments when he admitted to gut-deep fear, not that he would ever tell her that. He'd added more coverage, and the sheriff had men keeping an eye on the house, too.

But Galen knew very well that if Wolf was determined enough, he'd get to Rose and the kids. And he hadn't yet—so that meant Wolf just wanted to keep them all frightened. In limbo.

Enduring the same fear Galen's parents and his Callahan cousins' parents must have felt, all those years ago.

Chapter Eleven

When little Mack Galen came home the next day from the hospital, the Christmas spirit finally hit Rose. "My boy is home!" she exclaimed. "It's almost a merry Christmas!" She smiled at Galen and reached to take her son in her arms. "Although it breaks my heart that your baby brother is still at the hospital. I'll go see him tomorrow." She looked up at Galen. "How is Riley?"

"Our mighty little mouse," he said. "Not much bigger than a mouse, squeaks like a mouse and sometimes makes faces like a mouse."

"Galen!" Rose gave her husband a reproving look, even though part of her wanted to laugh. She knew he was teasing—and yet it felt mean to tease about little Riley when he couldn't be home with the family.

"I'm sorry. I think of Mighty Mouse when I think of that sprig off the family tree. You know he's going to grow up to be a cattle puncher or a monster rodeo cowboy."

"I hope so." She gazed down at Mack, her father's namesake. "My sons are growing like tigers."

"Not tigers," Galen said. "They're growing like Callahans."

He handed her a bouquet of flowers—a beautiful knot of lilies and roses—surprising her. "What's this for?"

"Because you're my wife." He flung himself down next to her and grinned at the two babies she held. "A beautiful, patient wife."

"I'm not patient. Whoever told you that?"

"Fiona." His brow lifted. "Don't believe me?"

"There's no telling what your aunt might say about anything, but I doubt she ever claimed I was patient."

"She did say you had the soul of a saint to put up with me."

Fiona's earlier words lingered in Rose's mind. She'd tried hard not to think about them in the last week, but they were hard to forget. "Galen, remember when you said we didn't have to stay together? That you didn't want our relationship to be like your brothers', where they had to catch their wives after they'd gotten them pregnant?"

"Yeah. You see that my way worked much better. You're here with me, there's no drama and the kids are happy. We'll be a big happy family by Christmas."

"You do recall you mentioned something about us not needing to stay together if—"

He kissed the words right off her lips. "I know what I said to convince you it was safe to marry me, doll. But it was all a pretty trap, I'm afraid, and you fell for the shiny object. You're stuck with me." He took Mack from her and lay back with the baby on his chest. "Yes, stuck like peanut butter to the roof of a horse's mouth."

"Galen!" She laughed, relieved, happy to have her worries brushed away. But underneath the happiness, Rose knew she had decisions to make, for her sons' sakes.

"Here's the deal," Galen told Running Bear when they met in the canyons that night. "Everything went wrong. And when it went wrong, it went really wrong. I can tell my little wife is having serious second thoughts. There's got to be a way to fix all this, before it blows up in my face. My boys' first Christmas, my first with my wife, our first Christmas as a family, is in two weeks. The last thing I want is Wolf's shadow bunging up the holiday spirit. Help me, Grandfather."

Running Bear looked over at the canyons. They sat in his lair high above the deep arroyos. "They are coming closer all the time."

"I know." There were days Galen wasn't certain if he could hold them off any longer. "What do the cousins say?"

"That they're worried. They want to help you." The chief chose his words carefully. "They feel they've abandoned you to fight their battle."

"No." Galen shook his head. "My cousins didn't abandon us. We understand the mission. They have families."

"You, too, have a family. Which is what makes them feel maybe they've asked too much of the Chacon Callahans."

"Not to worry." He'd been on many missions, some longer than this one. "None of my siblings have mentioned leaving Rancho Diablo. Some go, some return. In the end, we all stay." He didn't mention that he'd felt Rose's doubts recently. She hadn't said anything, but he knew her well enough to figure out what she was thinking. Her fears were clearly written on her face— had been since the night her father and home had been attacked. Fear for her father, fear for the children—fear in not knowing what was to come.

She was the bravest woman he knew outside of his family, and he could clearly feel that fear had become part of her thoughts. "I'm going to have to do something about Rose."

"I know." Running Bear nodded. "In time, you will know, too."

"That's not very helpful." Galen sighed. "On another topic, I think Fiona and Burke need to leave Rancho Diablo. I'm not comfortable with them here. Fiona has done her time. She needs to move on, to relax and enjoy life instead of being a convenient target for Wolf." Galen studied the burned land across the canyon, the blackened earth clearly visible. Egyptian legend claimed that the phoenix burned every five hundred years, only to rise from the ashes better than ever.

Maybe they would all rise, strong and fearless.

"I wish he'd pick on one of us," Galen said, "instead of a helpless old woman, and my pregnant wife. Seems very small of him."

"Be careful what you wish for."

Galen snorted. "I could never regret wishing that it was me instead of Fiona or Rose. My wife is very different now, and it's not just that she's a new mom. Where she was once fearless, she now tastes fear."

"Yes." Running Bear nodded.

There wasn't much Galen could do about that at the moment except protect her and his children, and Mack. He still had Sawyer on duty, along with a rotating team of other guards. "I don't understand what happened. Rose has nothing to offer Wolf. It's his same old bag of tricks."

"The object is to let us know we are always in danger, that he has eyes in many places."

"Which is why I think Fiona and Burke need to go. With fewer targets, we're not as interesting to hunt."

"Will you be the one to tell Fiona she has to leave?" Running Bear asked. "I would not relish that task."

"I know she wouldn't thank me for my opinion."

"No. And you wouldn't find any lunch bags or cookies with your name on them for many moons." Running Bear nodded. "Be careful of her feelings."

"What's Storm's role in all this?"

"Fear. Same as what you now know. He, too, has a family he wishes to protect."

"So he's a victim?"

"We all choose to be a victim or not."

"Great." His grandfather was being even more sphinxlike than usual. "Is he on our side or Wolf's?"

"He was on no one's side except his own. Now his nieces have been used against each other. If you fear for someone, fear for Storm. He has a lot to lose."

Galen's mouth twisted. "You're asking me to feel sympathy for a neighbor I never really trusted."

"How can you know the man unless you wear his shoes?"

Galen stood. "Should I mention to Fiona that perhaps she and Burke should consider—"

"At your peril." Running Bear waved a hand at him. "Look for the answers inside yourself. Meditate. You can't solve everything yourself. In the tribe, you learned to trust each other and your guide. Don't turn away from that now."

Galen blinked at the sudden cloud of dust that swept up the canyon, obliterating the ledge where his grandfather had been seated. Minutes later, only some swirling dust let him know his grandfather had been there, that his spirit still remained.

Galen went off to find his family. If Running Bear was all about teamwork, then it was time to meet with the team.

THE FAMILY MEETING was a tense, uncomfortable affair. No one passed tumblers of whiskey around that night, no one laughed or teased him about being a new father. Everyone was on edge after the recent attacks.

Grandfather was right: the enemy was getting closer all the time, now almost lodged in their psyches.

"Decisions must be made," Galen said. "Hard decisions, but it's time to face them."

His brothers and sister looked at him, their faces dark with concern, as they had been the night he'd gathered them together to tell them their parents had gone.

That had been a hellish night. There'd been so much he couldn't tell them—and yet explaining to them they were now on their own had been hard enough. He'd borne that burden carefully, jealously, for all these many years, a fierce caretaker of his family then as now.

Only he and Running Bear knew where Carlos and Julia, their parents, were. Witness protection was a mysterious refuge, and the secret would go with him to his grave. He couldn't tell his family anything—and yet now he had to tell them that the very mission was in jeopardy.

"I know you know that Rose and her father, Mack, were attacked the night she went into labor," Galen began. "Sawyer Cash and Somer were involved."

"Which I haven't quite wrapped my head around," Jace said. "I thought Sawyer was long gone and never looking back."

"She was. She called me about work. I had a job for her." Galen leveled a gaze on his brother.

"You could have mentioned it," Jace said.

"No. I could not have mentioned it. It was not my secret to tell." Galen laid a map he'd drawn of Rancho Diablo, the canyons and their neighbors to the east and west out on the table. "This map details our position. Here you have the burned land we've recently purchased—"

"You've recently purchased," Jace interjected.

Galen turned to face his brother. "If you have a problem, share it."

"I don't think you have a right to keep an operative's location secret from us, for one thing," Jace said.

"Sawyer's life is her own. Anything else?"

His brothers and sister stared at him curiously.

"We should all be part of the land purchase," Jace added.

Galen shrugged. "I've done what Grandfather asked. I know that originally Fiona offered that land as incentive for all of us to marry—"

"Which you've most conveniently done," Jace stated.

Ash reached over and pinched him. "What is your problem tonight?"

"He's jealous," Dante said.

"Angry," Tighe said. "In a knot over Sawyer."

"That's just too bad," Ash said.

Galen knocked on the table to bring their attention back to the matter at hand. "All personal issues get left outside. We have to attack this problem as a team—a tribe—or we're gonna lose."

Jace sat back, grumbling under his breath. Galen continued. "On this side is Bode Jenkins, a neighbor we haven't talked to much, but who's related by marriage to our Callahan cousins. That's a safe zone." He marked that area in red. "On this side is Storm. We would like to call his ranch a safe zone, but at the moment we have to color it gray. Storm's working his own demons, and there's no telling how Wolf's going to try to play that, however unfortunate for Storm." Galen marked that area off. "Back here are the canyons, and beyond that, the new land parcel. All to be marked blue, no longer safe. We know that," he said, looking at his siblings, "because Wolf's men have infested the area."

He took the blue marker, and over Rancho Diablo drew slashing lines. "Call this area Rancho Diablo Hell, because that's what it is. Underneath the ranch we may have our own man-made canyons, built by and maintained by the cartel. The same folks our parents and our Callahan cousins' parents were fighting against. We know they have tunneled under the acreage I just bought. The farmer was too old and didn't maintain his land well. Never saw anything, and I doubt he even left the house much."

Galen turned to gaze at his family. "We discovered this underground world less than a year ago. I've talked to the sheriff, and he's bringing in the Feds. We have no choice. I can think of no other way to save Rancho Diablo and our families."

His siblings looked astonished.

"You can't make those decisions on your own," Jace said.

"I had counsel," Galen answered. "And after the shooting at Mack's place, I knew we'd run out of options. Wherever we go, Wolf's going to have us covered. That's his message to us. Even if he has to use our own employees, we won't be safe. That's not so much a problem for me as it is for you, and your wives."

"What does that mean?" Ash demanded.

"It means that I took care of all of you when you were young. But I can't protect you anymore," Galen said. "The enemy is strong, so strong that even the strongest among us may be in danger."

"Pessimism never won the day," Ash retorted. "Let's not be dramatic, Galen. We can take care of ourselves."

"True, but not, perhaps, our families."

His sister shook her head. "Nobody has been seriously hurt."

His brothers stared at her.

"You can't mean that," Sloan said. "We've had wives held prisoner for months in Montana. Aunt Fiona was kidnapped. We're barely hanging on here, Ash. Galen's right."

"I don't know that he is," Jace said, obviously still smarting from the whole issue with Sawyer. He glared at Galen. "Why isn't Running Bear telling us all this? We should hear it from him."

Galen shrugged. "Ask him yourself." He turned back to the map. "Given that we're surrounded, the Feds are treading lightly. We're to stay in the background, not get in their way."

"I've never trusted the damn government," Ash snapped, and her brothers stared at her again. "Why should we rely on outside forces?" she asked. "I say we go it alone."

"I vote with Ash," Jace said. "This is family business."

Dante stood, finally taking the whiskey decanter and

pouring himself a drink. "We stay together. Whatever decision is made by the majority, we live as one."

"I can't," Ash said. "Galen's wrong. He's gone around us and made several decisions without discussing them with us. Hiring Sawyer as his personal guard, now bringing in the Feds…" She glared at him. "You're not the patriarch of this family, Galen."

"I'd say he is," Tighe said, taking the bottle from his twin and pouring a drink for himself. "As the brother whose wife was held prisoner by Wolf for several months, and who still smiles at the sound of lightning, thanks to the party favor Fiona ignited on Wolf's den, I'm agreeing with Galen. We need help."

"That makes you the tie-breaker, Falcon," Ash said, "unless Dante cares to go against Tighe."

Since Tighe and Dante were so close as twins that sometimes it seemed they had one head, Galen wasn't too worried.

"Not yet," Dante said. "I'm waiting to hear more of the story."

Galen raised a glass to Falcon. "Speak, tie-breaker."

"We have no choice. This isn't just Rancho Diablo, it's the Unites States," Falcon said. "If a cartel has run tunnels under the land, it's our duty to report it to the appropriate law enforcement agencies. Which may have the ultimate effect of driving Wolf back—or better yet, out, altogether."

Galen nodded. "That's the way I see it." He looked at Ash and Jace. "It may be our best hope."

"Our land will be torn up by federal agents," Ash said bitterly. "They'll leave trash and bother us. Our operation will no longer be our own. We won't be *free*."

"This isn't *our* land," Galen said. "We protect it for

our Callahan cousins. And ever since Wolf took his first hostage from among us, we haven't been free. He's taken women and he's kidnapped a child. What more must we sacrifice?"

"All," Jace said. "Does Grandfather agree with what you've done?"

"I've talked with him. And I've also told him that I think Fiona and Burke must go away. For good."

Six pairs of eyes stared at him.

"You mean after Christmas, right?" Ash asked.

"I mean as soon as we can pack their bags. It's not safe here for them," Galen said.

Ash stood and went to the door. "You're wrong. Everything you're doing is wrong. You should be with your wife, taking care of her and your new babies. You're making decisions that show your fear."

She left, and the room fell silent.

Galen turned back to look at the map. There were no other options.

Chapter Twelve

"What are you doing?" Galen demanded, and Rose let out a little squeal as her husband walked into the room. He was big-shouldered and handsome, and at the moment scowling at her.

"I'm going to see Riley." She pulled on her boots with an effort. "You said he might come home today. I'm going to see if I can spring him."

"You need rest, honey." Galen came over to shoo her back to bed, and Rose dug in her heels.

"I'm fine. I don't need rest. I need to see my son. It's the holiday season, and he doesn't need to be alone in a hospital without his brothers and his parents."

"I'll go." Galen watched as she pulled on her warm coat. "I'll get Riley. Please stay here. What if you slip and fall on the snow or an ice patch?"

"Then it will hurt like crazy." Rose refused to be deterred because of her husband's worrying. "I appreciate that you're concerned about me, handsome," she said, giving him a quick kiss on the lips and wishing she could linger, "but it's not necessary. I've walked in snow before."

"Not after you've had three sons. My sons." He sat

on the bed and put his arm around her. "Who's going to watch little Mack and Ross?"

"Dad's on deck for babysitting. And he's pretty happy about it. I told him I'd only be gone thirty minutes." She closed her eyes as Galen began scattering a leisurely trail of kisses down her neck. "It's not going to work, you know. In fact, it's only going to make me want to run out the door, since I won't be cleared for letting you do sexy things to me for a while yet."

"I can still kiss you." He sneaked a hand under her coat.

"No," Rose said. "I'm well aware you're trying to sidetrack me. And I'm leaving now to see my son."

Galen got up. "I'll drive."

"I thought you had to be at the ranch." Rose looked at her big strong husband and thought how lucky she was to be married to him. He had his overprotective moments—like now—but he was so sexy and sweet she couldn't wait to get the green light from her doctor.

"I do need to be at Rancho Diablo." He buttoned her coat. "But my wife wants to take a drive."

"Dad says the roads aren't bad." Rose stretched up to kiss him. "You don't have to take me."

"I want to see our son, too. Besides, they might release him, and if they do, we'll bring him home together."

Rose smiled. "That would be wonderful, wouldn't it? A Christmas miracle."

"The only one I want." Galen went out the door. "Give me five minutes to warm the truck up for you."

She smiled, falling a little bit more in love with him all the time.

"THERE'S SOMETHING I HAVE TO TELL YOU," Galen said, after he'd helped his wife into the truck.

"Okay." She looked at him expectantly, a small smile on her face.

I could look at her all day.

"I've informed the family that I believe Fiona and Burke need to leave Rancho Diablo."

"But have you told Fiona?"

"No. I think she'll understand."

Rose settled a red knitted hat on her blond hair. He forced himself to pay attention to the road and not his sexy wife.

"I think she won't."

He grunted, knowing Rose was probably right.

"When do you think this should happen?" She looked at him, then applied some lipstick that matched her hat. He felt himself responding, and reminded himself sternly that he had another few weeks to go before he could enjoy his wife in the bedroom.

"As soon as possible."

He now had Rose's complete attention. "You're not saying she and Burke should leave before the big charity ball next weekend? The dance she's had every year without fail, except last year?"

"That's exactly what I'm saying."

"I don't envy you when you tell her. She's going to say you're a traitor nephew."

"The thought has occurred to me." He didn't relish it. "Maybe you could tell her."

Rose laughed out loud. "No, husband. You can take care of your own dirty work."

"Fiona might see a woman's point of view—"

"No, handsome. I aim to stay on the good side of my

in-laws. But thank you for thinking of me." She went back to primping.

He was halfway into the doghouse. Might as well go all the way. "Here's the thing, babe. I think you and the children need to move, too."

"Nope." She didn't stop fluffing her hair as she said it. "Goodness, it feels good to get out of the house! Galen, I want to do some Christmas shopping today, if the doctor doesn't release Riley. My heart will be so broken. Not that I think retail therapy will help all that much, but I feel our Christmas tree is a bit bare without gifts under it. And I want a Christmas ornament that commemorates our first year together as a family. I hope we'll all be together for the holiday…." she said, her voice drifting off.

He wanted so badly to tell her it would be all right, wanted to make it right. Wanted to tell her that Riley would be able to come home, and that the three-times-a-day visits to the hospital to see him would be a thing of the past. Rose looked so sad he could barely stand it. Galen could tell she hadn't given his words about moving away a serious thought, so he figured it was best to keep her on happier subjects. "Christmas shopping for what else besides an ornament?"

"Galen! For the babies! And Dad. Of course, the babies want to shop for their father, too."

"I don't need anything," he said gruffly, thinking he had everything he needed. A wife and three sons—what man wouldn't feel complete?

He was more complete than he deserved to be. Somehow he had to make her understand the danger she faced now. It was something that kept him up at night, fear eating at his soul. "I know you're ignoring what I said about moving, and I don't want to rain on your parade while we're going to see Riley, but we'll have to talk about this, gorgeous."

"I'm not going into hiding."

He didn't know how to respond when she put it in such stark terms.

"I've had a steady stream of aunts, uncles and well-wishers at Dad's house. No one is going to get to us. Our house has become a regular hotspot, and I have a calendar full of folks who want to either bring meals or watch babies. There's no way I'm giving that up just because you're having a tiny bit of dad blues. And for the record, I think Fiona's going to hand you your head when you bring up your idea."

Rose leaned over and kissed his cheek as he pulled into the hospital parking lot. "My suggestion is you take a deep breath, relax, do one of those meditation poses you like and try to realize that you're not the man who's responsible for a bunch of young, parentless teens anymore. I can take care of myself, and I know Fiona can." Rose hopped out of the truck, eager to see her son.

Galen followed, knowing full well his brave wife meant every word she'd just said—which didn't do a whole lot for his comfort level.

AN HOUR LATER, Rose's dreams were dashed. She let Galen guide her back to the truck, her heart heavy with sadness. "It won't be Christmas without little Riley."

"I know." Galen stopped in the parking lot and hugged her. It felt good to stand in the shelter of his arms, but nothing could truly make her feel better.

"I really had my hopes up. He looked so small lying there. Oh, Galen, I just feel so sorry for him." Rose burst into tears, unable to hold them back any longer. From the moment the doctor had said Riley was still under-weight and needed further monitoring, she'd been bat-ting back her emotions.

"It's going to be okay, babe. It will all work out. This is best for his long-term health." Galen rubbed her back, comforting her, but she knew he felt it, too. His voice was raw when he spoke, even though he was doing his best to reassure her.

"I'm so sorry." She pulled away, looked into his eyes. "I know this is just as hard on you as it is on me."

They stood silently a few moments, holding each other, and then Galen finally spoke.

"Babe, I know very well that if the house hadn't come under siege that day, if you hadn't gotten up to try to help your father, the babies wouldn't have been born so soon. You might even still be carrying them. I'll always blame myself for that, but—" he kissed her hair and stroked it "—I can't allow anything further to happen. I want you and the children and Mack to go away."

She cried again, unable to help the tears as she pressed against Galen's chest, wishing she wouldn't ever have to let him go. He murmured soft words to her, but as she stared across the parking lot at the hospital where Riley was, where he'd be for Christmas, Rose knew Galen was right. It wasn't fair. It felt horrible to know that she would be separated from him, and the children from their big strong father. But it wasn't a destiny any of them had chosen, and Galen was doing his best to protect them. She'd noticed even little Riley had his own guard out-side the neonatal nursery, even though she hadn't said a word to Galen when she'd realized with maternal dread that the guard was for her tiny, struggling son.

Even though there were many blessings she could

count—and did—it wasn't going to be Christmas without them all together as one happy family. Certainly not the Christmas she had dreamed of.

With a heavy heart, she let Galen help her into the truck. Rose was sure that the worst feeling she'd ever experienced—and likely ever would—was when they drove away from the hospital, leaving Riley behind.

Chapter Thirteen

"Psst!"

Galen sat up at the urgent summons, staring into the darkness as he reached for his gun on the nightstand.

"What is it?" Rose asked sleepily beside him.

"Nothing. I'm going to get a snack. Go back to sleep." He got out of bed, pulled on some jeans, grabbed his 9 mm and moved stealthily to find who had whispered in their bedroom. Mack never did anything like that, and the babies were asleep in the room with them. The skin on the back of Galen's neck prickled as he walked into the kitchen.

His sister sat at the table, munching on cookies.

"Ash! What the hell?"

Her platinum hair was wild about her face, making her appear more pale than usual, more fey. She waved him over to the table, as if her breaking into their home at 4:00 a.m. was a normal occurrence.

He slid the gun lock on and laid the weapon on the table as he took a seat. "You could put the coffee on if you're going to rob a guy of sleep."

"Good idea." She got up and headed to the coffee-maker. "Fiona and Burke have left. I'll let that be the starter topic."

"Left?" Maybe it was sleep deprivation from having

newborns, and a wife who was upset that he wanted her to go away, but Galen's brain was moving like a turtle. "Why?"

"She heard about the 'perfidy of your plans.' That's what Fiona said." Ash grinned at him. "I doubt very seriously you'll receive a remembrance in her will."

"That's fine. Where'd she and Burke go?"

His sister finished fiddling with the coffeemaker and sat back at the table. "Isn't the purpose of being in hiding having nobody know where you are?"

"You know. I know you know. Don't fool around."

Ash sighed. "She's very upset with you."

"I'm okay with that." Everybody was upset with him. "I'm growing armor against those emotions."

"Tough guy." Ash bit into a cookie. "She sent these goodies along, but she instructed me that you're not to have any. They're for Mack and Rose, because you're a treacherous nephew." His sister beamed. "I do believe I'm the favored one now."

He took a chocolate chip cookie and bit into it, anyway. "Nobody makes cookies like Fiona."

"She's moved into Storm Cash's place."

His jaw dropped. "What?"

Ash nodded. "Clever, huh? She can keep an eye on everything, and get away from your big opinionated self. That's a direct quote."

"That hardly protects her from Wolf."

"Fiona said to tell you when you brought that up—and she said you would—that she and Burke can take care of themselves, and had for many years before you decided to insert your Captain Cowboy notions into her life."

Galen groaned. "Who told her?"

"I did. I said that you'd discussed it at the meeting."

Ash joyfully munched another cookie. "I really think there were sparks shooting out of her head when I repeated your poorly chosen opinions."

"Thanks." He shook his head. "Her going to Storm's isn't what I had in mind. I meant *go away* go away."

Ash shrugged. "I'm annoyed with you, too, you know. Let that be on the record. You bought land I intended to win. I was going to call it Sister Wind Ranch. I support *why* you had to do it, but I already told you I want naming rights."

If he could, he'd give his siblings every damn acre if it would get him some peace and quiet.

"I'm following orders from the chief. Believe me, I didn't see myself as the owner of a burned-out ranch house and several acres that's home to traffickers." Or worse.

"Well, la-di-da, brother. You've got a real snakes' nest out there now. We've had a couple drone flyovers, a few reporters and a rash of Fed types crawling all over the land ever since you let the sheriff inform the authorities that we have a wee cartel problem in the area."

Drones and reporters were bad. "I expected the Feds, the ATF, maybe some border patrol…but not drones."

"The reporters are worse than the drones." Ash rolled her eyes. "They ask questions. We all agreed that we won't talk to them, not yet. It's a shame. Used to be so peaceful at Rancho Diablo."

"It was never peaceful at Rancho Diablo, Ash. Sorry to burst your bubble. We've been barely holding off attacks for a couple of years now."

"Well, it's too late to put the genie back in the bottle, for sure." His sister looked at him. "We think you should come back home. I know you have a lot going on here, but we need a manager at the ranch. You've always managed us." She glanced toward the bedroom. "I know the timing could be better."

"The timing could be better for everyone. I'm sure the timing wasn't perfect for our parents, either." He drummed his fingers on the table. "Wolf probably knows to strike exactly when we're stretched the thinnest."

"With next weekend being Fiona's pet project—the ball, in case you forgot—"

"No one forgets Fiona's Christmas party," Galen interrupted. "She wouldn't let us."

"Any luck in getting your wife to go into hiding?"

He shook his head. "Between Rose and Fiona, I'm pretty unpopular."

"That's not just limited to Rose and Fiona," Ash teased. "And yet you're the only one who played his cards right, Galen," she said wistfully. "I give you heck about everything, but this one thing you've done exactly right."

He looked at his sister, surprised by the unusual praise. "*What* did I do right?"

"You cut to the chase. You got married, then had children," Ash said softly. "Organized and focused, just like you've been all your life. Our brothers had to race to catch their women, but not you. Always steady as a rock."

It hadn't felt very steady to him at the time. Sometimes it felt shaky. He was acutely aware that his wife didn't completely trust him since he'd mentioned her going into hiding. "It's not as smooth as it seems. I don't think Rose is too pleased that her life feels like it's been caught in a whirlwind since our marriage."

"Rose knew what she was getting herself into."

"Maybe." It was one thing to know it, and one thing to live the life of a warrior.

Ash rose. "She'll cheer up in a bit when the baby blues wear off."

"Baby blues?" One of them was blue, but he was pretty sure it was him and not his wife. She was certainly the stronger of the two of them.

"Hormones. I think a couple of the Callahan wives suffered from them. Some ladies get them worse than others, so I hear." Ash grinned. "I don't intend to find out."

If Rose was blue about anything, it was that tiny Riley might not be home for Christmas. Galen rose to walk his sister out. "So no luck with Xav, the canyon cowboy, I'm guessing?"

"I quit trying to break that particular stallion to saddle a long time ago," she said. She tucked her light hair into a black cap and zipped her tight black jacket at the door, then patted his cheek. "You might want to be at the ranch tonight. Things really are cooking out there."

He glanced toward the bedroom. "And what do you propose I do with my wife and kids?"

"I don't know. What do you think our parents, and the Callahan parents, did with their partners and kids when things began to get out of hand?" She slipped off into the darkness, and he barely saw her walk away. He listened for a car to start up, or a vehicle of any kind, but there was no noise other than the wind gusting, blowing the snow off the roof. He shivered, forcing himself to relax against the sudden cold stealing over him.

He waited another few minutes, listening for any sound, but Ash was long gone. She had stolen away, unnoticed by any shooter that might be out there, which didn't surprise him.

Going back inside, he picked his gun up off the kitchen table and went into the bedroom to snuggle his wife for another thirty minutes, before it was time to get up and help Mack with the chores. Galen shucked his jeans and slid into bed, pleased when Rose butted her backside up against him and pulled his arm around her waist.

"I don't want to freeze you," he whispered, wishing he could do more than hold her.

"Feels good. Go back to sleep," she said. "I'll yell your ears off in the morning."

He nuzzled her neck. "Yell? Not kiss?"

"No." Rose sighed. "I heard every word you and Ash were saying. And I'm not happy with you, handsome. You go to sleep, get some rest and dream sweet dreams of me and the babies living right here in this house, with or without you."

THE MORNING OF FIONA'S Christmas ball dawned dark with rain. It slashed against the windows and seemed to pour from the sky in a ceaseless torrent. Rose looked out at the water saturating everything, and shook her head at her husband. "The weather's dreadful."

"It's okay. We'll move everybody inside the auditorium. I'm sure Fiona has half a dozen backup plans."

She watched Galen place his hat on his head and his gun in the holster at his back. "I'll miss you, but I don't envy you getting to go dancing tonight."

He glanced up at her. "I won't be dancing. I'm just going along to keep an eye on things."

Rose poured him a thermos of coffee for the road.

"Has Fiona forgiven you yet for suggesting she needed to leave Rancho Diablo?"

He looked out the window at the storm. "Not so much. I didn't expect her to. Nor was I expecting her to just move to the next ranch over. But I get zero respect from all the Callahan women." He sat and pulled Rose into his lap so he could nuzzle her neck.

"I respect you," she said.

"Sure you do." He kissed her with more heat, and Rose felt herself falling for her husband's charms.

"I'll get the okay any day now," she said, loving it when she felt Galen pause behind her. She turned to face him and wound her arms around his neck. "It won't be much longer."

"I'm patient. You just heal properly, and then I'll—"

A baby's wail reached them, and a second wail joined in. Rose giggled. "You were saying, husband?"

"I was saying," Galen said, pushing her gently off his lap, "that this is going to be a very busy Christmas. I'll help you feed them, and then I've got to run. Not that I want to leave you." He glanced at the fireplace. "I'll make sure there are enough logs inside today, too, for the fire."

He was always so sweet, so considerate. Rose followed him into their bedroom. She picked up baby Mack, and he cradled Ross to his chest, then changed his small son's diaper while she began to nurse his brother.

"I love watching you do that," Galen said.

She smiled a little sadly. "It just never feels right to me that Riley isn't here to be with us all. It's like a family that's missing an important piece of its heart."

"Before you know it, we'll all be together." Galen's brows knit together suddenly.

"What is it?" Rose asked.

"I don't suppose if I offered to send you to Hawaii or someplace warm for a few weeks, that you and your dad would take the babies and go?"

"No. And quit worrying. Nothing's going to happen."

"I'd feel better."

"No, you wouldn't. You'd miss us. Go enjoy the ball and get your mind off of everything for a night."

"That's exactly when Wolf will strike—when I get my mind off everything."

Rose frowned. "Galen, I understand that the ranch and its problems weigh on you. But I think it's important for you to leave all that at the door when you come home. When you come *here*."

He nodded. "I'll try."

"Okay, then. I'm going to think about Hawaiian beaches right now and relax for both of us." She didn't look at him again as he laid little Ross next to his brother to nurse. Instead she closed her eyes and tried to think of sunshine and sand, coconut-scented sun-tan oil and satiny waves that rolled in and out with a hypnotic, timeless rhythm.

An image of the magic wedding dress popped into her mind instead. Rose's eyes flew open.

Galen grinned at her.

"I know what you're thinking," he said as he lounged on the bed, watching her feed his sons.

"You do?"

"Yes. You're thinking one day we'll move these boys into their own little bunk beds, and then it'll just be me and you. And you'll seduce me like you did at Rancho Diablo—"

She laughed, startling the babies. "Go away. Please. I can handle it from here."

"I wouldn't dream of leaving now. This is the best part." He leaned back, a sexy grin lighting his face. "You're absolutely beautiful when you take care of my boys."

She felt a little embarrassed. "Anyway, I wasn't thinking about you at all."

"Whoa. Easy on the ego, wife."

"For some reason, I was thinking about the magic wedding dress," she confessed. "Which is kind of silly, because I don't remember ever having a great urge to wear it."

"Oh, that gown gets every Callahan bride eventually." He didn't look disturbed by that fact at all. "I just didn't bother to succumb to the dress."

"I didn't think it was the husbands who succumbed."

He put his hands behind his head. "My brothers had no choice but to succumb to Fiona's fairy tale."

"I think Mack is done. He wants his diaper changed. This is one child who doesn't like to be wet for very long."

"Don't blame him a bit." Galen got to work, efficiently changing his displeased son, then pressed him to his chest. Mack calmed down instantly, and Rose thought it had to be wonderful to be held against Galen's broad chest, feeling warm and protected.

"So the magic wedding dress really isn't magic?" Rose asked. "It's just a fairy tale Fiona tells to help you guys get to the altar?"

"Not me," Galen said cheerfully. "I don't need fairy tales. I deal in reality only."

She held Ross tenderly, stroking his head with one

finger while he nursed. "Then how is it that the dress looked different on every one of the Callahan brides?"

"Fiona's extremely handy with a needle," Galen said. "Don't let her feed you that malarkey about it transforming itself to fit each bride. There's not a dress on the planet that could be magic to all the brides the Callahans have seduced."

"Seduced?"

"That's what they did," Galen said. "Almost to a man. I, however, didn't put the cart before the horse. If you recall, I asked you to marry me almost immediately. Once I make my mind up, nothing stops me." He looked really proud about that.

"I always wondered about you and Somer," Rose said. "I'm pretty sure she had a thing for you at one time, and sometimes I thought you might not have been entirely reluctant."

He shrugged. "Now you're telling yourself a dark fairy tale. Somer's not my type, beautiful."

Rose nodded, knowing he was being honest. "What ever happened to Somer? I truly did consider her a friend."

His gaze slipped away, as did his relaxed demeanor. "I don't really know."

Rose's eyes widened. She looked at her sexy husband, his face turned away, focused completely on Mack as he held him. "Galen?"

He looked at her. "Yes?"

"Tell me."

A long sigh escaped him. "Rose, the night that she knocked your father out—"

"We don't know it was her. She says it wasn't."

"The only two operatives on the ranch that night were Sawyer and Somer," Galen pointed out.

"Dad says he's sure a man hit him."

"Let's not talk about this while you're feeding my son." Galen got up, put sleepy Mack in his bassinet. "It can't be good for his digestion. I want sons with happy digestion."

She laughed. "Galen, does this child look like he's suffering any kind of distress?" Rose realized what she'd said, and her heart grew heavy again. "Riley needs to be here so I can feed him with his brothers."

Galen kissed her on the forehead. "Peace. Calm. Happiness, babe. Only happy thoughts when you feed the boys. A man really enjoys his mealtime—didn't your dad ever tell you that? It's the only time of the day a guy really needs to have his soul at peace."

She tried not to smile and failed. "Before you go…"

"I really don't want to leave you."

"I know."

He knelt down next to her and rubbed her arm as he gazed at his son.

"Just keep in mind that I feel almost positive Somer was set up," Rose murmured.

His dark blue eyes met hers. "Set up?"

She nodded. "It makes sense."

"By who?"

"Wolf. Through Storm. That's what I think," Rose said, feeling a strong need to defend her friend. "None of it makes sense otherwise, Galen. I just don't believe in my heart that she would try to hurt my father."

He nodded. "Okay. I'll admit I like your loyal side. You're a sweet thing."

Her brows furrowed. "I'm not being sweet. I'm telling you that the conclusion everyone has drawn is too obvious. Somer needs to be let out of jail at once. I know that's where she is, and that you don't want me thinking about it. But she doesn't belong in prison. She didn't do anything wrong."

Shaking his head, Galen rose, then put his hat back on. "It's not up to me, babe. Are you sure you're going to be all right? I have to get out to Fiona's shindig. I'm so happy I'm not up on the block this year, I can barely contain myself. I'm going to enjoy needling Jace and Ash about doing their civic duty as Fiona's raffle bounty."

"Along with about ten other brides. I want a full report when you get home," Rose said eagerly. "I heard that even Storm Cash is on the block this year, and that Lulu Feinstrom said she's ready to outbid any woman who dares to make an offer on him. And that if a bidder from out of town wins him, Lulu vows to go on the date with them."

"I can see you admire Lu's attempt to keep her man," Galen teased.

"You remember that tonight when you're around all the pretty, man-hungry ladies wearing their costumes and waving their money around."

"It's okay, beautiful. You got the cream of the Callahan crop and you didn't have to spend a dime for it."

Rose sniffed. "Careful, Callahan. Your head may expand so much you won't be able to fit through the door."

He winked at her. "I wasn't going to bring this up, but I have a long memory—and I recall you bidding handsomely for me year before last. I was very disappointed when you let Sawyer outbid you at the end. Just between you and me, that was the least fun date I ever had. It wasn't really even a date—more of an outing. I'm pretty sure she was just using me to get to Jace. Truthfully, I think you would have been a lot happier if you'd taken me home with you that night. We would have probably been a year ahead in our relationship." He grinned. "Still, in a few weeks, I intend to make up for lost time with my sexy wife."

Rose got up to put Ross down next to his brother, and kissed both their heads. They settled into their blankets, happy and satisfied. She went to her closet, retrieved a new blouse. Came back out and stood in front of her vanity mirror, and brushed her hair. Pulled her top off and then her bra. Galen watched her hungrily in the mirror.

"I think I'll take a shower," she said. "I'll see you later. Wake me when you get home."

In the bathroom, she pulled off the rest of her clothes, turned on water hot enough to steam the bathroom and knock the chill out of the air, and stepped into the stall.

A moment later, Galen joined her, wrapping his arms around her from behind. "You tempt me, Mrs. Chacon Callahan. I may stay here for our own party."

"You're going to be late," Rose said, turning to kiss her husband. He had a very obvious situation going on, and Rose put soapy hands around him to solve the problem. Galen groaned and held her to him, kissing her forehead, then her lips.

"I'll be late, but I'll be smiling," he said. "Don't think I don't know that you're trying to soften me up about speaking to the sheriff about your friend being in jail."

Rose melted against him, enjoying the feel of her husband close to her again. "I just want you to keep an open mind."

He kissed the top of her head. "I hope I don't regret it, but I'll mention your theory."

"Thank you."

Galen kissed her long and sweetly, brushing his hands gently over her breasts, holding her against him, and Rose thought everything was just about perfect.

Once Riley came home, they'd be a family—and then everything *would* be absolutely perfect.

Chapter Fourteen

"Looks like a hundred men or more over there," Galen said. Wanting his grandfather's advice, he'd stopped here first, and stood with Running Bear at the edge of the canyons, looking through binoculars at the land he was in the process of finalizing paperwork on. "That's a lot of men in uniform. Part of me thinks Rancho Diablo is safer now that we'll be up to our ears in law enforcement. The other part of me knows we've stirred up a hell of a hornets' nest."

Running Bear shifted beside him. "Now that reporters are here and the whole country's watching, Wolf will find another way to achieve his goal."

"Yeah, but what?" Galen looked toward the neighboring ranch. "This is exactly why Storm wanted to sell to me. He realized he'd gotten caught between a rock and a hard place. In the end, he chose to bail out, and I understand."

"Your aunt and uncle are going to buy Storm's land. They've decided they want a place of their own. They've put in their own paperwork to stop you buying the acreage."

Galen blinked. "Buy it? Why?"

"You told them to leave."

"You and I discussed it, decided them leaving would be best, Grandfather. I don't think either one of us meant they should move next door."

Running Bear nodded. "Fiona does as she pleases."

"Did you post guards on Storm's place?"

"Yes. Fiona sent them off. She said they were needed elsewhere, considering how thin Rancho Diablo's resources are stretched."

Galen sighed. "I'm not having much luck convincing Rose to take the kids and her father and go away for a while until everything cools off."

"Because it might not cool off for years, and Rose knows this. She had to make a choice. Stay with you or go. She doesn't want to take her children away from their father. You automatically assumed she would go, because you've seen that with your own parents. Rose sees little danger to herself, or she would not have allowed you to drop her into that cave. How many women would do that?"

Galen smiled at the memory. "I could barely get her to come back out. She was like an archaeologist down there."

"It is not that your parents, or your Callahan cousins' parents—my sons and their wives—were afraid. They knew what they were battling. Mack has kept Rose safe. She doesn't recognize fear because she's never been—"

"Out of her ivory tower," Galen said, with dawning comprehension.

"Something like that. She has not met real danger. So she does not know it."

"She wasn't even really afraid the night her father was attacked. She'd pulled on her boots to go outside and warn us." Galen looked at the men and horses on the land he'd bought, and had an idea. "Wouldn't it be safe at Rancho Diablo now? Now that there's reporters and all kinds of activity? She'd really like to be here with me, if she could." A family all together—that was what his wife wanted more than anything.

"Less safe. Every single person—even a reporter— could be the enemy in disguise. Before, we knew who the enemy was. Now," Running Bear said, pointing to the men scattered across the canyons, "a disguise will be easy. Now there is no safety for anyone."

"I hadn't thought about that." Galen's stomach tightened. "Any of those men could be on Wolf's payroll, too."

"I see many faces, but few I trust."

Galen turned away, mounted his horse. "Now what?"

"Only the Great Spirit knows."

"Have you ever noticed that all of this seems to be heating up under my watch?" Galen glanced toward the main house. The seven chimneys of Rancho Diablo rose majestically in the distance. "All this trouble coming here now. Maybe I'm the hunted one you told us about, Grandfather," he said softly. He turned to look at Running Bear. "Am I?"

The old chief shook his head. "I do not know. I just know the prophecy. The hunted one will bring danger and destruction to Rancho Diablo. Will you do that?"

"I hope not." Galen had tried to do only good.

Yet so much had turned out badly.

GALEN WENT OVER to see Fiona and Burke, needing to set things right between him and his spry aunt before her big charity event. He felt bad that she was living in

Storm's house, and it was eating at his conscience that they'd had harsh words between them.

"I'd like to say it's nice of you to come by," Fiona said when she opened the door to him, "but you've probably come to annoy me, so I'll skip the pleasantries, nephew."

He stepped inside Storm's house, the first time he'd ever crossed this threshold. "Come home, Aunt Fiona. You don't belong here. And you don't want to buy this place."

"You wanted me to leave, so I did." She went into the kitchen and began loading cupcakes she'd baked into containers for carrying.

"I didn't want you to leave to go next door. I wanted you to leave Rancho Diablo to be safe. There's a difference. This isn't any safer."

He felt his aunt's glare. "Nephew, Burke and I are doing fine. We were fine over there, but we're just as fine here."

"Says the woman Wolf kidnapped not too long ago. Aunt Fiona, you know very well you're on Wolf's bad list because you sent his hideout to the moon." Galen sat on a leather-covered bar stool to try to further his case. "Doesn't Burke see the situation as dangerous?"

"Burke disagrees with you as I do," she said sharply. "But then we're fighters, Burke and me, if you recall. We were fighting for the cause in Ireland before we came to take care of the Callahans, and before you ever came to Rancho Diablo."

He sighed, sensing he was in very hot water with his aunt and not getting out of the pot anytime soon. "Fiona, I wouldn't feel so strongly about this if I didn't love you so much."

She waved a spatula at him. "We can take care of ourselves."

It was the same thing Rose said. "I hate being the bad guy—"

"Then don't be," Fiona said.

"Wolf just attacked our home, sent Storm in to keep you locked down," Galen pointed out.

"And look how that turned out for Storm. I believe I acquitted myself well that day, as did Rose. I really think you're not giving your wife sufficient credit for her survival instincts."

Shaking his head, he got up and snagged a cupcake, earning himself a stinging smack with the spatula. The cupcake was worth it, and he raised it in salute to Fiona as he departed from Storm's kitchen.

"Just a minute, nephew," she called after him.

He turned at the door, and she brought him a glass of milk. "You'll want milk to go with that. And I expect I'll be seeing you tonight at the ball, ready to be a help and not a hindrance?" She raised a brow that lifted nearly to her white hair, pulled back in what she called a "bird's nest" hairdo.

"You know I'll be there, Aunt Fiona. I only want the best for you and Burke."

"I'll expect you to act like it this evening. Now off with you. I have a thousand things to do and no time for idle chatter about nonsense."

He left, milk and cupcake in hand. Fiona wasn't totally furious with him if she was feeding him—but she hadn't forgiven him, either.

The most important females in his life were deeply annoyed with him at the moment, but he didn't know what to do about it. They all had to leave.

He'd never forgive himself if Wolf got to anyone Galen loved. The thought was entirely too terrible to bear.

ROSE MADE SURE the boys were still asleep as she lay their baskets next to her father. Mack sat on the sofa in front of a nice fire, watching a television show. "Thanks for agreeing to watch little Mack and Ross, Dad. I won't be gone long." She tucked a wool scarf around her neck, buttoned her coat and headed to the door.

"I don't mind watching my grandsons. I'm just not sure you should be going out tonight," Mack said, his face lined with worry.

"It's okay. I want to be with Riley when they feed him. So I won't be gone more than an hour."

"What if Galen calls?"

"He can call my cell. But he's at Fiona's charity ball, so he'll be busy. Bye, Dad." She left before her father could voice more objections.

No one really understood how horrible it felt to leave one son behind, while the others were at home with family, surrounded by love. It was the Christmas season, and yet Rose didn't feel happy. She felt sad and somehow lonely, as if a huge piece of her was missing.

It was too hard to believe that Riley wouldn't be home with them Christmas morning.

She drove to the hospital and signed in at the desk. In the nursery Riley lay in his bassinet, surrounded by nine other babies and several nurses. Yet tears jumped into Rose's eyes because he seemed so small, and despite the company, so alone. She knew it was silly, because Riley was a baby; he'd never know he was separated from his brothers. When he was grown he wouldn't remember that his first holiday season had been spent in a hospital.

She hurt so bad it felt as if the pain never left her chest, as if strings that tied her to her child stretched but never let go. Would never do so until she could hold him in her arms, place him in his own bassinet at home.

The doctor saw her through the glass, came out with a smile.

"Hello, Mrs. Callahan."

"Good evening, Doctor."

"Your son's doing fine. He's put on another couple of ounces."

"Really?" Rose felt some of the darkness lift away. "That's great news!" It was the best she'd had in a long time.

The doctor smiled sympathetically. "Four whole ounces."

Rose felt hope bloom inside her. "You don't suppose Riley might come home for Christmas, do you?"

"I'm much more hopeful than I was a couple of days ago. And I believe in miracles. Good night, Mrs. Callahan."

"Good night." Rose watched as Riley was gently stroked by a nurse. Tears of joy jumped into her eyes. "I believe in miracles, too," she murmured, and turned to leave.

Out of the corner of her eyes, Rose saw a dark form. She turned to look at the stranger watching her, and he stared back at her. Obviously, the man was one of the guards Galen had hired; he had on a dark blue uniform with a security badge. Rose relaxed a bit and then walked out into the parking lot. The wind picked up, teasing her hair with damp, cold gusts. She couldn't wait to text Galen and tell him the good news.

GALEN STARED AT the text from Rose, his heart literally seeming to jump for joy. Riley may get to come home for Christmas! He's gained four ounces!

That would be the best Christmas present ever—and moreover, it would make his wife the happiest woman on the planet. She'd asked him to take her Christmas shopping, but he hadn't wanted to tire her. Now he felt the Christmas spirit himself, and it had nothing to do with Fiona's ball tonight.

He gazed up at the moon, grateful beyond words that his son was beginning to thrive. It had been such a hard battle to see that tiny body behind the glass, and know there was nothing he could do to help him. How powerless he'd felt. Galen had fought many battles in his life, had seen many hard things, and as a physician, he was no stranger to both the frailty and strength of the human body.

It had been so devastating to know that his son hovered between life and death, and only the spirits of his ancestors and his own fight for survival were his tools. "My strong-hearted son," Galen murmured. "Like a lion."

He wrote, What a miracle that would be, and sent the text, his soul no longer heavy and foglike. He felt strong again, hopeful.

After he helped at the charity ball tonight, he was going home to his wife and children. Tomorrow he would take her shopping in Tempest—Santa Fe, if she wanted—and let her browse to her heart's content.

He heard a sound behind him as he dismounted from

his horse, and glanced around at the shadows. His imagination flared with suspicion. As Grandfather had said, there were so many people on the ranch now. The tunnels really had been a shock to the Diablo community as a whole, not just the Callahans.

Galen took the saddle and blanket off his horse, replaced the bridle with a lead rope. Washed just the saddle area because of the cold, keeping the bath brief, then dried the horse thoroughly before putting a nice warm blanket on him for the night. A groom came to take over, and Galen nodded his thanks. He stepped out of the barn, noticing that the snow around the entrance was well-trampled despite the fresh flakes falling. There was red splattered about, drops of it, a strange thing to see in glare of the yard lights. He bent down to look at the spots, and pain exploded in his head.

ROSE SMILED AT the text she received from Fiona. Tell Galen duty calls.

She wrote back, He won't let you down. Try to keep the ladies away from my husband.

He's not here. Late as usual, I might add.

Rose shook her head. Galen had left Tempest hours ago. She couldn't imagine why he wasn't already helping set up at the Christmas ball. Glancing at the clock, she went to check on the babies. They'd been fussy for the last hour, which was strange for them, because neither Mack nor Ross were fussy babies. "What is going on with you two tonight? You've cried more in the last hour than you have since you were born!"

She rubbed their tiny backs soothingly and they relaxed a little, curling toward each other a bit more. They were so darling and sweet. Rose couldn't wait until Riley came home and the three of them could sleep together. She'd made an appointment with a photographer to come and take a family photo the day after Christmas—just in case Riley did get released from the hospital.

She jumped when her cell phone rang. "Hello, Fiona."

"Is Galen there?" his aunt demanded without social niceties—which was very weird for chatty Fiona. Rose glanced at the digital clock beside the bed. It was ten o'clock.

"He's not, Fiona. He left hours ago. Isn't it time for the bidding?"

"Yes! And that's why I need him here. Someone's got to help me corral these folks. We've got a bumper crop of attendees, and Galen's organizational skills are needed. There are brides and bidders galore."

"Okay," Rose said, trying to soothe the obviously frazzled aunt. "Have you tried his cell? Because we texted each other not that long ago. Maybe an hour."

"Of course! He's not answering, he's not picking up. If you hear from him, will you tell him he's out of my will if he doesn't get here pronto?"

The phone went dead, and Rose smiled. "Your great-aunt is in quite the froth tonight. Kind of like you guys. Must be something in the air."

But the babies were calm for the moment, so Rose went to the other room to try Galen's phone again. He didn't pick up, but sometimes cell service was spotty in some areas of Diablo. She sent a text, and settled in front of the fireplace with a scarf she was knitting for him for Christmas.

Thirty minutes later, she received another frantic text from Fiona. Hear anything from my tardy nephew?

Unease crept into Rose. She glanced at her father

when he walked into the den to toss a couple logs onto the fire.

"Galen's not at the charity ball."

Mack looked up at her, then went back to situating the logs the way he wanted them in the grate. "Probably got caught with some ranch duties. The place is crawling with Feds and reporters and gawkers, too, I imagine, with the shindig tonight. Folks from out of town are always curious to see the Callahan castle."

Rose nodded. "I know you're right, and yet I can't help being uneasy. And the babies were restless tonight. They're not usually cranky."

Mack came to sit beside her, patted her leg. "Babies fuss sometimes. I wouldn't worry."

"Husbands don't go missing," Rose said. "At least mine doesn't."

"Now that is a bit more of a curiosity," Mack said. "Galen's pretty good about staying in touch, I agree. He usually rings me up if he can't find you."

Galen had been known to send up a flare if he didn't get a response from her in five to ten minutes. She'd teased him once about being a worrywart, and he'd said that she was his wife and a free spirit—he couldn't trust what she might do when he wasn't around to keep an eye on her. Then he'd kissed her, and lured her with his rascal smile, and she'd dragged him off to bed to do things to him she knew he liked.

"I'm scared, Dad."

"Well," Mack said, thoughtfully rubbing the ankle he'd rested over his other knee, "I can call Sheriff Cartwright over in Diablo. Tell him we're missing a Callahan. No doubt he and his deputies are at the party. He'll probably have seen your man."

She combed through every possible scenario of why Galen might not be at the ball. "I know he had every intention of helping Fiona with her big event. It's the Callahan pride and joy, besides their weddings." The more she talked about it, the more strange it seemed that Galen wasn't with his aunt. "Even if a horse was foaling, or the house was on fire, he'd call his aunt. Those two get on each other's nerves, but in the end, they're like two hands that need each other to clap."

He patted her knee and rose. "I'll give Cartwright a buzz. You sit there and knit that scarf and stay warm. Everything's fine, I'm sure, but caution is even finer."

Rose told herself nothing was wrong—but fear settled over her, telling her something was very, terribly wrong.

Chapter Fifteen

Galen looked sourly at the seven thugs surrounding him in the dim cave. He could feel a goose egg knotting at the back of his skull, and his feet and hands were bound.

When he got free, he was going to kick some uncle ass—no matter what Running Bear said about not hurting Wolf.

"You're the first true Callahan we've gotten our hands on. My brother Carlos's bloodline," Wolf said gleefully. "We've been hunting big game, and you're just about the biggest."

Wolf's right-hand man, Rhein, grinned. "Only Ashlyn or Running Bear would be bigger. Still, you're a trophy fish, Callahan." Rhein kicked dirt at Galen, sending puffs of dust over his boots. Rhein had a hearty laugh at his expense, and Galen decided right then and there that his was yet another butt that needed a thorough kicking.

"Don't know what you're going to solve having me as your guest," Galen said.

"It's very simple." Wolf squatted down to where he lay on the ground. "One of you knows where Carlos and Julia are. Maybe you even know where Jeremiah and Molly are. The cartel wants blood since my brothers turned them in, and they've patiently waited for it."

Galen was the only one who knew where his parents were; even Fiona didn't know that. Running Bear knew, but he would die before he revealed his sons' location. And Galen was no different. "I always thought my parents were dead. And I know nothing about Molly and Jeremiah. I never met them."

Wolf smiled. "I have the strangest feeling you're lying, nephew."

"What difference does the past make?" Galen asked. "According to a few law enforcement agencies, there are enough tunnels under that farmer's property to open up interstate commerce. You have no reason to still be concerned with my parents. Clearly, you've managed to achieve your goals."

Wolf laughed. "You didn't really think the cartel had gone away just because my brothers had big mouths? They didn't solve anything when they informed on them. The cartel just went underground, got stronger."

"So what's their game?"

"This is the easiest route to move goods that they want to get to market."

"Drugs," Galen said flatly.

"Drugs, weapons, other things." His uncle smiled. "Once I take over Rancho Diablo, this will be a thriving hub for a business far more profitable than selling a few head of cattle a year."

"You won't get Rancho Diablo."

"I'm Running Bear's last son. Of course I'll get Rancho Diablo. You have no claim to it. None of you do. It's in your Callahan cousins' hands, thanks to Fiona. But they've been gone for years, letting you do their dirty work. I'll eventually get it." Wolf smiled. "Don't be sur-

prised when I do, because I told you it would happen.
And it will be easier than you think."

Galen made no comment. Wolf couldn't understand
the bonds of family. Galen knew his siblings felt the
same as he did: they were proud to stand with each other.
The Callahan cousins would do the same for them.

Anything less than a fight would never be an option.

MACK CAME INTO the kitchen, glanced at the teapot Rose
had on the table and the fresh bread and blackberries
she'd put on some plates nearby. He sat down and took
the mug she offered.

"It's after midnight. Aren't you going to sleep?" Mack
asked.

"I can't, Dad. I'm worried about Galen. I think about
Riley. I want my family together." She shook her head.
"I figure if I fall asleep, the babies will wake up soon
enough and need to be fed. Might as well not lie in bed
and stare at the ceiling."

"Heard anything from Diablo?" He helped himself to
some of the fresh-baked cinnamon bread.

"Just that it was a bumper year for bids. The bride-
a-thon was very popular. Jace drew quite the crowd,
and apparently Ash was the knockout favorite." Rose
smiled. "Somer called to say that Galen had gotten her
out of jail, which she wanted to thank me for, but she's
released on her own recognizance and backed by Galen,
so it had nothing to do with me."

Rose planned to show Galen just how much she appreciated him listening to her and believing her about
Somer's innocence. She loved him all the more for his
kindness and loyalty on her behalf.

"Ash was so annoyed to have to participate she could

barely be nice to the bidders" Rose added. "But apparently at the last second, an anonymous bid came in that knocked all the others out of the running."

Mack smiled. "Anonymous?"

"Fiona thinks Ash rigged it, that she had a friend phone in with funds Ash put up herself. She swears she did no such thing, and can't imagine who the knockout bid could be from."

"I guess it doesn't matter in the end. Fiona gets her funds for her projects in Diablo, and Ash doesn't have to sit through a date with a guy she doesn't want to talk to."

"I guess so." Rose got up to look out the window, even though it was so dark she couldn't see a thing. "A woman from Tempest won Jace, but I haven't heard the name of the lucky winner yet."

"I'm sure you'll hear plenty soon enough."

She couldn't imagine why Galen had never shown up for his family's big social event. The planning always took months, and since he'd been a participant in the bachelor raffle before, he knew very well how much the Christmas charity ball meant to Fiona. "It's just not like Galen to be AWOL."

"Sheriff Cartwright's got everybody keeping an eye out for him. They'll find him. I know he's never very far away from you and the boys, so I'm not worried."

Rose couldn't be comforted by her father's words. Turning away from the window, she sat again, trying to breathe through the knot that had formed in her throat. Her nerves were strung tight as wires.

"So you're talking to Somer?" Mack looked at her. "Are you that convinced of her innocence?"

"You say she didn't attack you."

"It wasn't her," he agreed. "But Galen's still suspicious."

"Galen's suspicious of everyone in general, and I can't blame him." Her stomach rolled as the minutes drifted by. Somer had also said Galen never made it to the ball, but no one had mentioned seeing him at Rancho Diablo before that, either.

Which meant he hadn't made it there.

"Would you mind if I went to Rancho Diablo, Dad?"

"I think you'll feel better if you do." He got up, reached for her coat. "But I want you to be safe on the roads."

"I will be." She let him help her put the coat on. "It's not that I think I can do anything—"

"I know."

"It's the waiting—"

"I know," Mack said. "I feel the same way. Go."

"There's frozen breast milk—"

"Rose, honey, I know. I raised you, and I can watch two little babies for a few hours. Go." He grinned at her. "The three of us fellows are going to bond a little while you're gone. And there's a couple of football games I taped that I wanted to review," he added with a teasing smile. "Me and the boys are going to take in some games and get our strategy on for the next playoff. It's important that they learn early about football, rodeo and ranching."

She kissed his cheek. "Thanks, Daddy."

"It's fine," Mack said, following her to the door and walking her out to her truck. He helped her knock some of the snow off it and made sure the windshield wipers weren't frozen. "Galen's going to yell my ears off for letting you go, but a woman's got to do what a woman's got to do."

"He'll probably yell my ears off, too." She couldn't worry about that right now. "I'll be back soon."

ROSE DIDN'T BOTHER going to the ball in Diablo's town square. She went straight to Rancho Diablo. If Galen wasn't at Fiona's big party, then he was at the ranch and out of reach.

The sheriff could have overlooked the attic or the basement or a hundred other nooks and crannies in the huge castlelike mansion. Galen's siblings would have been more thorough in their search, but Ash had been at the ball being bid on, as had Jace, and the rest of the brothers had been stretched thin.

Rose would feel better if she could check Rancho Diablo for herself. She combed his room, the attic, the basement and everywhere in between. The house was quiet with everybody at the ball. In the living room, a Christmas tree glowed with tiny colored lights and tons of ornaments—a testament to Fiona's love of the holidays.

Rose went out to the barn and checked for his horse. It was in its stall, which meant he was somewhere on the massive property.

Maybe she was overthinking this. Wolf had been inclined to kidnap women—and Galen wouldn't be an easy target. He was big, wide-shouldered, strong.

An uneasy tickle ran along her spine.

She dialed Jace's mobile phone.

"Hello?"

"Jace, it's Rose."

"Hello, my sister-in-law. I did the family proud. The ladies bid me up to—"

"Jace," she said, interrupting his bragging, "have you seen Galen?"

"No, I haven't, and Fiona's none too pleased. She was expecting all hands on deck tonight."

"His horse is in the barn."

"That's odd," Jace said. "Hey, Ash! Do you know where our knuckleheaded big brother is?"

"Galen?" Rose heard her say. "He's not been here all night, and the plucky aunt is fit to be plucked."

"I'm really worried," Rose said. She glanced around in the dark, seeing a few ranch hands walking around, but none she recognized. "It's not like him to not be in touch."

"Where are you?" Jace demanded.

"At Rancho Diablo."

"Alone?"

"Yes," Rose said. "And I feel like something's wrong…."

"I'll be right there," Jace said. "Stay in the house and lock the doors."

He hung up, and she hurried to the main house, locked herself in and waited, her heart pounding. Maybe her mind was playing tricks on her after the stresses of the past few months. Her father had warned her in the beginning that life with a Callahan wouldn't be easy—but actually, life with Galen was very easy in so many ways, one being that he was never hard to reach by phone. As Mack had said tonight, if Galen couldn't get hold of her for five minutes, he rang her dad to check on her.

She sat in front of the fireplace near the Christmas tree and tried to concentrate on the pretty ornaments and the many splendidly wrapped presents. Most were for the Callahan children, given that there were so many kids in the family.

Not that there were many at Rancho Diablo lately. Wives and children tended to get moved away, for safety's sake.

Not me. I'm coming right back here. I'm no safer in Tempest than I am here—and my sons won't be, either. The family that lives together, stays together.

Galen wouldn't like it, but at least if she was here, she wouldn't worry all the time. It was the not knowing that was the worst.

Jace burst through the back door just then, frightening her half to death as he dashed into the den, with Ash following behind. "Have you lost your mind? Galen's going to gnaw on you if he finds out you were here unprotected," his brother exclaimed.

"Don't whine, Jace. She had a gut instinct, a flash of sixth sense, and acted on it." Ash hugged Rose. "We'll find him."

"I want you to take me to the cave," she said, and they stared at her.

"Not *the* cave?" Jace said. "I can't do that. Galen will not only yell at you, he'll yell at me. And it won't be pleasant. It'll be worse than yelling. It'll be Galen on super—"

"I don't care." Fear raced through Rose. "Take me there."

"Not the cave you guys dangled Rose into a long time ago?" Ash asked.

"That's the one," Rose said. "There was a digging machine in it, and guns, and silver and gold, and a portrait of Running Bear. The alcove I saw was almost a storeroom. I realized that once I started thinking about it tonight," she said in a rush. "I have to know if they've taken Galen to that cave. Wolf doesn't know that we're aware of it, Jace. You know we made a clean getaway that night."

"You're panicked, I understand," he said soothingly. "But that's the last place they'd take Galen."

"Why?" Rose asked. "They don't know we found it."

"That's true," Ash said. "And it's close by."

"There could be hundreds of caves around," Jace pointed out. "There's a network of tunnels that were located on that land. The Feds have it all covered."

Ash muttered something that sounded like, "Feds, my foot."

Rose said, "But the law enforcement agencies don't know about that cave. It's not obvious from the sky or even standing on level ground, and we never told them. You can get into it only if you found that opening, and as far as I know, only you and Galen ever discovered it. There's another entrance, no doubt, but I didn't go far enough back, because you and Galen were hyperventilating about me being down there."

"True," Jace said. "I've never seen Galen in such a twist before." He thought for a minute. "Ash and I will go. You stay here, Rose."

"I'm not staying here! I'm the only one who can fit down there." She tightened her scarf in preparation to leave.

"Ash could fit if you can," Jace said.

"Yes, that's true, but you can't hold the rope by yourself," Rose said. "You need me."

"You're not helping anchor a rope," Ash said. "You've just had babies and stitches and stuff. We should call Sloan or Falcon, Jace."

"No," Rose said. "It's too dangerous to have too many Callahans in one place."

"What about you?" Ash said. "You're as much a Callahan now as we are."

"Wolf isn't after me, or he would have already grabbed me. He's done grabbing wives and children," Rose said with certainty. "He's after bigger game, especially with the Feds crawling all over this place. He had to ramp up his game."

"Galen would never allow himself to get taken," Jace said.

"He's a medical doctor, not an operator, as the rest of you are. He didn't have the extensive military training you got," Rose said, "remember? So his every thought isn't geared to watching over his shoulder. Besides which, we're both sleep-deprived and worried about Riley. Exhaustion and worry is not an optimum cocktail."

"She's right," Jace said slowly. "Galen was the manager among us, but he wasn't the hard-ass."

"True," Ash said. "We have nothing to lose by checking out the cave. Just to be certain. If nothing else, it will calm your mind." She looked at Rose. "I'm a firm believer in listening to those silent voices with warning shrieks."

Rose nodded. "Thank you. And if he's not there, I'm sending a dump truck tomorrow to fill in that stupid cave. I don't care what Wolf and his bosses would think or do about that."

She walked to the jeep, ready to ride. Behind her she heard Jace say, "Galen's going to kill us for letting her come with us."

Ash said, "Try to stop her. Go ahead, I'll love watching."

The brother and sister got in the jeep. Rose sat in the back, and no one said another word about her staying behind.

Chapter Sixteen

Rose knew that Ash and Jace were carrying pistols of some kind, and the gun rack had a complement of rifles on it, so she didn't feel unsafe. In fact, she wasn't afraid at all, except for Galen. She just knew her husband too well, and as Jace drove nearer where the cave was located, her uneasiness grew.

"I'll go down," she announced, and both Ash and Jace, seated up front, shook their heads.

"You stay in the car and man the wheel in case we need to make a fast exit," Jace told her. "If Galen finds out we let you anywhere near where Wolf and his men might be, he's going to excommunicate Ash and me from the family circle. It's serious business on this, Rose."

He pulled up close to the cave and glanced at his sister. "Let's make this fast. No need for us to get captured. I'd like to live to enjoy the little lady who won me tonight."

"Who was it, by the way?" Ash asked.

"I don't know, but it was some little sweetie from Tempest. I didn't catch the name. I don't care, either. Rose, you come sit behind the wheel, and leave the jeep running." He laid a black pistol on the dash. "This is in case you get any visitors."

She hopped out of the jeep and went around to the driver's seat. "Hurry, please. I know Galen's in trouble."

"All right, all right. We'll get our hammy-brained brother out of the rabbit hole. No worries," Jace said, winding a rope around his sister. "Many a time I've dreamed of dropping you into a cave and leaving you behind, sister dear. I just never thought I'd have the pleasure of doing it."

"If you leave me behind," she said, "you will so regret it."

He winked at Rose. "Sit tight, but be prepared to haul out of here."

She had no choice. It was enough that they took her seriously and were going to look for Galen, wasn't it?

Not really. Ash didn't know what Rose did about that sizable cavern. She knew she could explore it so much faster than Ash. Rose shut off the engine, grabbed the pistol and hurried after them.

"Wait for me!" she whispered loudly.

The two shadows ahead of her turned.

"What the hell are you doing?" Jace demanded. "Once the mission's begun, you can't go renegade."

"Sorry. I just don't see how you're going to lift Ash back out by yourself," Rose explained. "It took you and Galen both to get me out before. Since you won't let me anchor the rope, I'm going down. You and Ash should be able to handle my postpregnancy weight."

They looked at her. Jace shrugged. "Pregnant or not, you don't weigh much. Let's go, stubborn lady."

At the slice in the ground where they'd discovered the cave, Ash quickly tied the rope around Rose. "Hurry. We don't want to be found here, or we'll all get nabbed. Galen's going to kill us, anyway, for letting you do this, so don't get stuck and don't hang around and explore like you did before. Just in and out and gone."

"I know."

Jace handed her a Maglite and a decent-sized hunting knife. Ash said, "Just in case you find yourself in a tricky spot."

"Got it," Rose whispered, and put the knife in her boot, though she didn't think she could ever use such a thing. The pistol she kept in her hand, loaded and unlocked, just in case she found herself lowered into a trap. She took a deep breath to calm herself.

They began to let out the rope, and Rose squeezed through the opening. Once at the bottom, she stood, took off the rope and left it dangling.

There was no one in the large, dug-out space, but still she kept her gun ready. The front loader was still there, as was the painting of Running Bear. Nothing seemed to have moved. She worried about bats and spiders, but she could survive those. Galen was her primary concern.

And he didn't seem to be here. She'd been wrong.

She'd started to reach for the rope when she noticed a trail of what looked like blood, and shone the flashlight on it.

"Hurry, Rose!" she heard Ash hiss from above.

Rose followed the trail with the flashlight to the back of the cave, where it seemed to disappear. Maybe a wounded animal had crawled in here.

But then she felt air blowing on her hand, cold and yet warm at the same time, as if there was some kind of ventilation nearby. She felt the wall, expecting it to be sturdy—and a door squeaked open a fraction.

Her scalp prickled. Cautiously, she peered through the crack. Unable to see anything, she pushed the door open a bit farther. Nothing moved. It was quiet as a tomb in the space beyond.

It *felt* as if she were in a tomb. A sensation of danger swept through her. Rose inched forward, pushed by something she couldn't define, a feeling that she needed to go as far as she could—and then she saw the trail of blood on the floor again. She followed it, telling herself each footstep would definitely be the last. But then she heard a moan, and pressed forward once more.

She heard footsteps, and gasped. Something rustled in the corner and she sent her flashlight beam there. "Galen!"

He shook his head at her in warning. She ran to him, lying down behind him just as someone came along the corridor. Wolf swung a flashlight at Galen, and Rose shrank against his back.

"You're still here," his uncle said, and laughed.

Since Galen was not only bound but gagged, he couldn't reply. He pressed her against the wall behind him, and Rose lay very still.

"Something's not right about you," Wolf said. Rose's skin jumped with goose pimples as she prayed he wouldn't come closer. "I may not have gotten the spiritual gifts my brothers did, but I do know that you seem different somehow," he said to Galen. "Your eyes look hopeful. And fearful. I've never seen fear in your eyes." He shone the flashlight at Galen, and Rose held her breath. "I'm going to get some help to move you to another location," Wolf said. "I don't like the feeling I'm getting."

Rose heard footsteps as he walked away. She couldn't allow him to bring men to move Galen! Even if she got back out of the hole and somehow figured out a way to bring Ash and Jace here to rescue him, he'd be gone. Moved somewhere deeper in the tunnels, no doubt— and this time, she wouldn't know where to find him.

Rose reached around Galen with her pistol, took careful aim at Wolf's backside and fired.

He fell to the ground with a shriek, cursing. Rose grabbed the knife, quickly cutting Galen's bonds. He ripped the tape off his mouth, grabbed the knife and the pistol. She guided him to the entrance with the flashlight, both of them hurrying before Wolf alerted someone. He was rolling around on the ground in agony, but just before she passed through the door, Rose met his eyes.

She'd never seen such absolute hatred in her life.

"Hang on," she told Galen, and ran back to the tape and the ropes she'd cut off him. She took them over to Wolf, tying his ankles first, then his hands and finally she taped his mouth.

"Come on, babe!" Galen urged.

She stared down into Wolf's eyes. He glared back at her, his gaze fierce with hatred.

"I hate you, too. Don't mess with my family," she whispered, so that Galen couldn't hear her.

She hurried over to the door and went through it, Galen following close behind.

"When we get home, you're getting a spanking," he said. He tried to tie the rope around her, but she pushed him away. "You're injured. You go first."

"Just this once, listen to your husband." Galen put the rope around her and tugged at it.

Rose called, "Hurry!" to Jace, and he pulled her up. She squeezed back through the crack in the cave ceiling and ripped off the rope. "Galen's down there! I shot

Wolf, so pull fast!" she said, stuffing the end back down the hole.

The rope tugged again, and Jace and Ash leaned back, pulling hard. Rose slashed at the ground with the hunting knife, trying to widen the slice of earth enough for Galen to make it through. He was considerably larger than she was. She kept chipping away at the earth with all her might.

"Pull harder!" she told Ash and Jace—and suddenly, Galen's head came through the hole, and then his shoulders. Rose had never seen anything so wonderful, except when her children were born. She wanted so badly to kiss him, but there wasn't time. Galen's arms came through, and he pulled himself the rest of the way out.

"Hello, bro," Ash said. "Need help walking?"

"I'm good." He stumbled a bit, but kept up a fair pace. Rose ran ahead and started the engine, so Ash and Jace could ride shotgun and in the back, just in case they were pursued. Wolf's men would be on them any second. Galen dropped into the backseat with a groan, then checked the magazine of a pistol Jace handed back to him.

"You look like crap, Galen," his brother said. "Sight for sore eyes and all that."

"That's fine," Ash said, "Beat it out of here, Rose. Drive like you're being chased by your worst nightmare."

She was. She remembered Wolf's eyes as he'd stared her down—and knew she had an enemy for life. Rose drove as fast as she could, the jeep bumping and flying over ruts in the New Mexico ranch land, her blood chilled like ice.

"You two are in big trouble with me." Galen limped inside the house at Rancho Diablo and headed for some whiskey. "I want a shower, and then you," he said to Ash and Jace, "have some serious explaining to do. What were you thinking, taking my wife where Wolf could get her? She's not part of the mission!"

Rose reached to wipe some blood off his face, and he waved her away.

Galen glared at his sister and brother. "Wolf was there. He could have grabbed her." He pointed at Rose. "He *would* have taken her prisoner, except she shot him!"

"We heard the gun go off, and figured our girl had hit the target." Ash slapped Rose's hand in a high five. Jace reached for some whiskey and had the grace to look slightly ashamed, but Ash—no, shame wasn't an emotion she owned. That made Galen even hotter under the collar. He realized he was talking a bit out of his head, but just looking at his dainty wife—she'd had babies less than a month ago, for heaven's sake—just made him madder at Jace and Ash. "I'm going to shower. All of you stay out of my sight for a while. Then I'm calling a family meeting. I don't care if the party is just wrapping up in town."

Rose followed him to his room, watching as he stripped to boxer briefs that molded to his well-muscled legs. "You can't be mad at them. I made them take me to the cave."

"I *can* be mad at them." Galen stripped off, not able to look at his delicate wife. "I'm not happy with you, either. If you don't mind, I'd like to be alone."

"Fine. You can be alone all you like. But your back is bleeding, your face is cut, there's something oozing from your arm and I'm not so sure you're not going to need stitches in your head. Not that I'm a doctor like you, but that's just my opinion. Let me know when you're ready to go to the E.R. And by the way, you owe your brother and sister thanks. They're awesome. Later, you can tell us all how you came to let yourself get grabbed by your uncle."

She left the room, leaving him to fester in his bad mood. "I owe my siblings a swift kick in the pants," he muttered, and went to look in the bathroom mirror at the list of things Rose had mentioned he might need allopathic help with. He hadn't told her that at least two of his ribs were cracked, and there was a possibility he had a slight concussion. Maybe more than slight. He had a rocking headache from being punched in the head, and the kicks he'd taken to the ribs hadn't been sweetness and light, either.

But none of it was as bad as the fear that had hit him when he saw his sweet-faced wife poke her head through the cave door. He'd known Wolf was due back any moment, to come and check on him again, and the sheer terror that had held Galen in a vise grip was something he never wanted to feel again in his life.

Rose scared him to death. He didn't know how to deal with knowing that his wife was fearless. Absolutely fearless. "All I asked was that she stay home and look pretty. We talked about that," he muttered, checking the gaping wound over his eyebrow that one of Wolf's goons had opened up. "Just once I wanted not to be worried sick."

"You'll survive it," Rose said, coming into the bathroom and setting a bowl of ice beside him, and a tube of antibiotic ointment. "You can spend the rest of your life griping at me for everything. Won't bother me in the least." She gave him a saucy smile. "I'm going home now. Jace says he's on standby to run your cranky, unappreciative self to the E.R. Good night."

She left again, and Galen closed his eyes.

He'd married a warrior. And she was going to drive him mad.

"YOU SHOULD BE HAPPY Rose is so brave," Ash said as they gathered upstairs for the family meeting at about two in the morning. He'd been to the E.R. for a professional wrap of his ribs. His family could have done it, but they were being pains, saying that just for once, he needed to respect the opinions of others in the medical community. He knew they were worried about his headache, so he finally bent and let Jace haul him in for "proper" medical tests, evaluation and treatment.

But now he faced his family, fully prepared to let his temper fly. "I'm *not* happy she's so brave. I didn't marry Rose to be my bodyguard. You can't seem to get it through your skulls that she is my wife. She is a mother. I think I died a little when she came through that cave door." He glared at Sloan, Dante, Falcon and Tighe, who looked sympathetic. Then he passed a glare over Jace and Ash, who shrugged.

"If it wasn't for Rose, you'd still be in the hole, dude," Jace said.

"I'd rather be in the hole!" Galen went over to the whiskey and poured himself a stiff shot. He downed it, took a deep breath. "Look, try to visualize this. You're tied up and gagged. You're not sure you're ever going to see your family again. Suddenly, your petite wife, who's still breast-feeding your babies, walks through the door and shoots your uncle in the…" He glanced around the room wildly.

"Backside?" Sloan said helpfully.

"Keister?" Falcon said.

"Bum?" Dante offered.

"Gluteus maximus?" Tighe said.

"Getalong?" Jace chimed in.

They turned to stare at Jace.

"You know, like when you have a hitch in your get-along?" Jace said. "Jeez, tough crowd."

"Ass," Ash said, "Galen, your wife shot Uncle Wolf in the ass, and you're just going to have to get ahold of yourself. It's a kick in the pants, but you'll survive."

They all burst out laughing, as if it was the funniest thing they'd ever heard.

Galen collapsed on a sofa, shaking his head at the family he'd raised on his own. "I don't want to get hold of myself. She bound and gagged Wolf before we left, before I even realized what she was doing. And then she whispered something to him, and I'm pretty certain she wasn't inviting him to have tea and cupcakes with her one day." Galen drew a deep breath, wiped his brow where it itched from the seven stitches the doctor had put in. "Rose roped him like she was at a calf catch, and I was so astonished I couldn't move."

"Shouldn't have been moving, anyway," Ash said. "The doc said you have three broken ribs. Did the best you could, letting us drag you out of that cave. Had to have hurt like hell."

"That's not the point! The point is that my wife shot and bound the man who's been trying to kill our parents for years!" He got up, paced to a window. "Do you understand that Rose's life is now forever forfeit?" He looked around at his suddenly somber family. "And my children's?"

Jace got up, clapped him lightly on the back as he

poured himself a drink. "Nothing will happen. We won't let it."

"You think that." Galen looked out the window into the darkness. Knowing now what was out there, lurking. Waiting. "I didn't think I'd ever get attacked."

"How did that happen, anyway?" Tighe asked.

He sighed, feeling a bit stupid. "I had my mind on Rose. I was thinking about Riley, wondering if he could come home for Christmas." Galen stared down at the glass in his hand. "I was thinking about the blessings that have come my way this year, and I was praying for just one more—and then I got hit. The next thing I remember is being in the cave. I can't even tell you where the entrance to it is, because I didn't come to until I was being kicked awake by two of Wolf's men. I recognized Rhein, and the other guy we saw in Montana, but I don't know his name."

"Poor brother," Ash said, and came to give him a gentle hug that wouldn't hurt his ribs. "I'm sorry I teased you about Rose shooting Wolf's bony hindquarters." She winked at him. "We know this is a serious situation. We'll protect Rose with our lives."

His brothers murmured agreement. "I know," Galen said. "I know you'd do your best. But what I'm trying to say is that this is a test I don't want to try to pass anymore."

Chapter Seventeen

Rose looked up when Galen walked into the den in her father's house, and held up baby Ross to show him the new Christmas jammies their son was wearing. "Fiona said some of the ladies at the Books'n'Bingo Society made these," she said with delight, helping Ross model his new red velour pj's with a Rudolph the red-nosed reindeer embroidered on the front. "You can't believe the Christmas wardrobe the ladies made our three little guys."

Galen took Ross in his arms, and she picked up little Mack. "Nice stitches on your face. What other party favors did Wolf's crew give you?"

"Not many. It's not as bad as it looks."

"Yeah, it is." She felt the sturdy layer of wrapping beneath his ribs. "No holding babies for you," she told him, setting Mack down again and taking Ross back. "Dad! Can I borrow you for a minute?"

"I can hold my own sons," Galen said.

"Not for a while." Rose gestured him to a chair in front of the fireplace. "Sit, and I'll get you some coffee."

Mack came in the room and scooped up little Mack, who'd let out a few opinions at being abandoned while his brother continued to be held. "Now, now, little fellow," his grandpa said. "My namesake's clearly not going to be the quiet, retiring bookworm in the family. Come on, let's go find something tasty for me, and a bottle for you. Hey, Galen, nice work on your face."

Mack drifted out of the room, not bothered at all by Galen's sudden reappearance, and Rose smiled. "He's been awesome," she murmured. "A rock."

Galen nodded, but didn't reply.

So she didn't say another word. Clearly, he was still annoyed with her, and there was nothing she could do about that. She wouldn't change a thing she'd done, so he was just going to have to work himself out of his mood.

"I want you to go away," Galen said at last. "Surely now you understand what's at stake."

"I'm not going anywhere." Rose sat down with Ross and began to feed him. "I'm waiting on Riley to come home, and we're having Christmas right here." She smiled down at the baby and stroked his cheek. "He's growing so fast."

"Yes," Galen said, "and the thing is, moving—"

"I went to the hospital to see Riley," she announced, not caring that she interrupted her husband's soliloquy. She wasn't going to leave Tempest. And when she was ready to live back at Rancho Diablo—once Riley came home—she was going to do that, too. "He's such a handsome boy. I'll have all my sons home for Christmas, I just know it."

"Yes, about Christmas—"

"It's not going to do you any good to keep harping on me going away. I'm not going to do it," she told Galen.

"For the safety of the family, you're going to have to. I'm thinking maybe Australia would be a good option. And I'm willing to send Mack along."

She glared at her husband. "Australia! Clear around the world just because I shot your uncle?"

"Not only did you shoot him, I think you threatened him, although you haven't shared that conversation, and I doubt you ever will."

She shrugged. "We didn't say much of interest."

"I'm positive you weren't whispering pleasantries in his ear."

She turned away. "The children and I aren't leaving you. In fact, once Riley comes home from the hospital, we're moving back to Rancho Diablo." She refused to look at Galen; the hurt was too great. "I didn't expect thanks for getting you out of that underground tomb, but I didn't expect you to be hysterical about it, either."

"Rose—"

She put up a hand to stop his words, turned back around. "Galen, I did what I had to do. You do what you have to do."

Then she went to find her father, to ask him to take her and the babies Christmas shopping.

There *was* going to be a Christmas—no matter what Cowboy Scrooge thought.

As bad as things were between him and Rose—and he didn't think she planned to forgive him anytime soon for bringing up the idea that she and the babies would be safer elsewhere—he was comforted by the fact that at night, she still curled up against his back.

He was thankful every day of his life that he'd married Rose. She couldn't understand that she had to leave to keep herelf and their sons safe. He'd begun to plan their new home, looking into a place in Canada for his family, since she'd protested about going to Australia.

He didn't tell Rose of his plans—but eventually, he was going to explain to her that Wolf would never forgive her for what she'd done. The price on her head would be great; just thinking about it made his stomach cramp hard.

What she couldn't understand was that Wolf and his men—and the cartel—had been after the Callahans for so long that one little Rose wasn't going to stand in their way. She'd stabbed a knife into a nest of snakes, and they would come after her.

He decided to enlist Running Bear to help him explain the matter to his wife. If anybody could draw her a clear picture of the situation, it was his grandfather.

The chief could explain the mission. Galen really needed Running Bear's help, because the very idea of Wolf harming his wife or children evoked a fear he couldn't walk with any longer. He felt it tearing at his marriage, but he was caught between an unforgiving rock and an unending hard place, and try as he might, he couldn't see a compromise.

GALEN TOOK HIMSELF BACK to Rancho Diablo for two reasons: first, his darling wife refused to acknowledge his presence during daylight hours, which was killing him. He wanted her to see the matter his way—and he wanted her to love him again, the way she used to, with her sunny smile and her ready laughter that always seemed to be just for him.

That was pretty much a no-go with Rose at the moment.

Second, duty called at Rancho Diablo. So days, he worked the ranch. Nights, he'd watch the babies, even if his sweet wife gave him a wide berth. She called it giving him space until they worked things out.

He thought that translated to "give you your space until you come to your senses."

There really was no way to meet in the middle, because they both saw what had happened through different prisms. He was hoping time would give them clarity.

That was the plan—until Running Bear came to see him late one afternoon.

"Hello, Grandfather."

Running Bear nodded. "Seven stitches, seven Chacon Callahans."

Galen felt his forehead. "I never thought about it that way, but I guess I should be glad my parents didn't have twelve kids, huh?"

A crinkle appeared around Running Bear's eyes. "How do you feel?"

Lousy. He hated squabbling with his significant other. The bodily aches and pains were nothing compared to the hole he had in his soul. Rose liked to lie in bed with him and stroke the tattoo he had on his shoulder—the lightning bolt all his siblings had, symbolizing their unbreakable bond.

Rose didn't stroke anything of his anymore.

"I feel fine," Galen said. "Things will heal in a week or two." The ribs would take the longest. "Wolf's henchmen took me because they thought they could beat out of me where our parents are."

"You told them nothing."

"I have nothing to tell." Maybe their parents weren't even alive anymore. Running Bear might be shielding him and his siblings from another truth. It was hard to know with their grandfather. Sometimes Galen thought he'd go hunt his parents up—but then he'd put that fantasy away just as quickly. He didn't want to lead the cartel right to them.

"One day," the old chief said. "One day you will see them again. For now, be glad you married a woman you can be proud of. She is your true mate, the other half of your heart."

"She scares me."

Running Bear nodded. "I know. Carlos said the same about Julia."

"Did he?" Galen turned to look at his grandfather.

"A man wants to protect his woman. Of course, he was always afraid. But Julia did what she knew was right. Same as Molly, same as Fiona. And now Rose."

"Wolf will try to kill her. Rose says she only shot him with a .22, that the bullet was barely bigger than a peanut and certainly thinner. That Wolf was just being a crybaby, rolling around and squawking. She didn't aim for his legs because she didn't want to hit a femoral artery, and figured aiming for his fleshy bits was safest." Rose had even factored in a back pocket wallet, just in case. Chills ran over Galen. "She won't leave Tempest, either, and says she's coming right back here once Riley comes home."

"Do you know that Rose's mother died when she was very young?" Running Bear studied him. "She was always with Mack, who raised her like he would have a son. Rose has been hunting since she was small, can skin a deer faster and better than most men. Can cure the meat and cook it, catch a fish and clean it, and is trained in all things necessary for survival."

Galen rubbed his chin. "You're not making me feel a whole lot better."

"You have heard that before Mack was a sheriff—he was a Texas Ranger. When his wife died, he moved to Tempest to get away. But before he was a Ranger, he was a jarhead in Nam. That's what he calls it. The blood of a warrior runs thick in Rose. She never thought twice about wounding Wolf. She knew it was the only way the two of you were getting out of that hole alive." Running Bear pointed to an eagle swooping majestically over-head. "If she'd meant to kill him, she would have done so, Galen. Rose has excellent marksmanship."

He shook his head. "I don't want to hear any more. I want to know that my wife is at home knitting and taking care of my children. That's what she should be able to do, Grandfather. What normal wives do."

Running Bear pointed to the eagle again. "What do you see?"

"I see freedom," Galen said, watching the eagle return to its high aerie. "I see a fierce spirit."

"That's right," the chief said. "Do not speak words from fear. Speak only the truth you've always known."

Galen gazed at the eagle for another moment, absorbing the amazing sight of the great bird in harmony with the sky and the wind and the sun, before realizing his grandfather had disappeared.

Leaving him with only his words, as usual.

Galen got up to leave the canyons, and was surprised to see Somer riding toward him. He waited until she pulled up alongside him.

"Galen," she said, "got a minute?"

He nodded. "Sure."

"I want to thank you for speaking up on my behalf."

Galen shook his head. "I had nothing to do with it. That was all Rose. She insisted."

Somer looked sad. "I would never hurt her father. I think it's amazing that she trusts me enough to have you speak on my behalf."

Galen sighed. "My wife's pretty amazing. Thanks."

"She is." Somer slid off her horse so she could walk with him toward the main house. "Galen, I know who attacked Mack."

He looked at her. "Who?"

"Well, I don't know who, exactly. I don't know his name. But I can tell you he had a bad scar on his face. I'd know him again if I saw him."

A scar. There was only one man around with a remarkable facial scar, and that was Wolf's sidekick, Rhein. "Are you sure?"

"I'm sure. I ran across him one day when I was riding. I always exercise Gray in the afternoon when I'm off, in the morning when I'm not—"

"I know, I know," Galen said impatiently.

"And yesterday a man rode alongside me and mentioned that he was a reporter. There have been a few of those around," Somer said, and Galen nodded. "We're not supposed to give them any information, but what I thought was odd about this man was that he knew lots of details. Said he'd been talking to one of the neighbors, and I realized he meant Bode Jenkins, not Uncle Storm. But then it hit me that Bode has three Callahan granddaughters, and he wouldn't talk to anyone."

Bode was tough. The Callahan cousins had briefed Galen and his siblings about their gritty neighbor, told them if they ever needed anything, they could call on him. Every once in a while, Bode stopped by to chat with his ranch neighbors, but none of the Chacon Callahans would have known any significant details, much less mentioned them.

"What details did he know?"

"This was the giveaway for me," Somer said. "The man with the scar knew that Rose had been alone in the house that night. Even I didn't know if Rose was in Tempest or Rancho Diablo when Uncle Storm sent me out there to help Sawyer." She looked as if she wanted to cry. "Uncle Storm said that there were bad people everywhere and that he didn't want Sawyer guarding your property alone. That he'd never forgive himself if something happened to your family because of him." Tears filled her eyes now. "It's not an easy thing to know that you fired on your own cousin."

Friendly fire happened. No one liked to admit it, but Galen had been in the military long enough to know that things happened on occasion that no one liked. He shook his head, thinking about the tangled tale Somer was telling. "Rhein knew Rose was at home alone?"

"He asked me, as he was pretending to be a reporter, why you were rarely in Tempest with her." Somer wiped at her eyes. "I said I didn't know anything, and he said it was common knowledge that Rose was alone the night the attack happened on your place, and that somehow it was all related to what's going on here now at Rancho Diablo."

Anger fired deep inside Galen. "Why are they picking on Rose?"

"Because it worked," Somer said. "They got you, didn't they?"

He blinked. "Yeah. Actually, they did."

"No one knew where they took you. Only Rose figured it out. You would have been long gone and never found, if she hadn't," Somer pointed out. "They had a perfect plan."

She was right. And only he had the information they wanted.

"That means Rose is still a target. A prime target." Not just because she'd shot Wolf, but because she was the only one who'd gone against Grandfather's direct instruction that no one was to harm the man. Rose was a Callahan, but not subject to the same rules. If Wolf could get her, things would become ugly fast. Pain hit Galen in the gut as he realized how he'd let his stubborn pride argue with his sensible wife.

"Of course she's a prime target," Somer said, surprised. "She's a direct line to you. Even better, your three sons would be sure to get you talking. Right now there's no greater target in your family. But I'm sure you've got Rose guarded to the teeth. In fact, to make up for my part in what happened, I'd be honored if you'd allow me to be on staff in Tempest—"

"I need to find Rose. Right now."

They leaped into his truck and Galen took off like a bat out of hell, hoping he hadn't come to his senses too late.

Rose went Christmas shopping and baby shopping. There were a hundred things she wanted for the triplets' care—and she wanted gifts. Not that they would ever know there were presents under the tree for them, but somehow, a tree needed presents. Little giraffes and soft wind-up bears that played gentle lullabies. The presents were more for her than the babies, but Rose wanted her sons to have something from their parents.

She also wanted something for Galen, even if her

wonderful husband was being difficult. And then the
perfect gift occurred to her. It wasn't in a store, couldn't
be purchased.

There were two parts to the gift she envisioned. One
part was easy to schedule; the other, she had no idea
how to retrieve.

And Galen would freak out if she did.

The second-best option was the easiest. She went into
a shop to schedule the appointment.

Then she called Running Bear to ask his help for the
other. Galen would be mad—but it was exactly the thing
to mark their family's first Christmas together.

She headed back to her truck, holding two shopping
bags full of baby basics, towels and diapers. Mack had
already texted her with a report, so she knew everything
was fine on the home front.

A tiny teddy bear in a shop window caught her eye,
and she thought of little Riley. It was silly and whimsi-
cal, she knew; Riley would never know if a teddy bear
had been put under the tree to mark his place until he
could be home with the rest of his family.

Rose went into the shop to buy the bear anyway, and
ended up with three, each dressed in a different plaid
vest and beanie. "They're perfect," she told the shop-
keeper. "Thank you so much."

"Can I help you to your vehicle?" she asked.

"No, thank you, I'm fine. You're busy," Rose said,
looking around at all the shoppers anxiously trying to
find last-minute Christmas gifts. She went to her truck,
bent to open the trunk then turned when she felt a hand
touch her arm.

"Galen! What are you doing here?"

"Mack said you'd gone shopping. Thought you'd be

here." He put her purchases in the trunk. "I need to talk to you."

"Now?"

He nodded. "We could hit the coffee shop."

"I don't really need coffee. Can you just tell me what's on your mind?" He wasn't smiling, didn't look like her normally serene husband. Actually, he hadn't really smiled at her in a while—not since she'd shot his uncle.

He took a deep breath. "I know we're at cross-purposes on where you're going to live."

Rose closed the trunk. "We're not at cross-purposes. You're confused as to what a marriage is all about."

His jaw set. "I never made a secret of what life was like at Rancho Diablo."

"True. But I can make my own decisions. And I never made a secret about that."

He glanced around at the many passersby hurrying to choose Christmas presents and decorations. Snow gently fell, and Rose felt sad for the beauty of the moment that wasn't mirrored in their own lives.

"It's dangerous here, and dangerous at Rancho Diablo for you now."

"It was always dangerous. Just being your wife made it dangerous for me." She looked up at him. "It was you they kidnapped, Galen. They were probably at my dad's property trying to set a trap for you. Wolf's man, Rhein, just wasn't expecting to get in Somer's and Sawyer's crossfire." She smiled. "As a matter of fact, I consider that night a blessing."

Galen looked uncertain, and maybe a little annoyed. "It was no blessing. You wouldn't have gone into labor except for what happened that night."

"You don't know that. Maybe we both just need to accept that we don't agree on this matter. Now, I'm going to finish my shopping." Sadly, she turned and went into the bakery, deciding she'd grab a pecan pie for Mack, and maybe some cinnamon cake for breakfast.

Galen followed her into the bakery and dropped into a chair, looking so unhappy that Rose felt slightly bad about her harsh words. In his brown cowboy hat and sheepskin jacket, boots and jeans, he looked sexy and wonderful—her husband, after all the years she'd waited for him—and the way he was gazing at her put splinters in her heart. "Could we get two cups of coffee and two slices of cinnamon cake at that table?" she asked the girl behind the beautifully decorated counter. It was Christmas—she and Galen should be happy. They had so many reasons to be.

She sat down next to him. "Let me try again, because I don't mean to come across as uncaring." She looked into his eyes so he'd know she was completely sincere. "I'm sorry I shot your uncle. I know everything changed when I did that. Although it's not going to sound like much of an apology when I say I would do it all over again." She put her hand on his arm. "Galen, Wolf was coming back. He was bringing henchmen, and they were going to move you. My gun had a silencer on it, and it was a .22—just an equalizer, really. Your uncle was being a big baby about a wee piece of lead in his fanny. According to your grandfather, Wolf was back at his mean tricks the very next day. So if you want me to be sorry I did it, I'll say I'm sorry, because I don't want you to be upset. But just know that I'm pretty sure if I had to choose again between getting you out of there and burying a small reminder in your uncle's posterior, I'd let my gun leave a calling card."

A reluctant smile turned up one corner of Galen's mouth. "That's pretty skewed thinking, angel."

"It's all I've got. It's how I see it. You don't think I was going to let Wolf take you off where I might never find you?"

"I would have gotten away somehow."

"I know that. And part of me thinks that maybe it's your pride that's stinging more than anything."

He shook his head. "What bothers me, beautiful, is that you painted a target on you and my children. He's not ever going to forget what you did. You can't do anything else to put the babies in jeopardy."

"You think I'd do *anything* to put them in jeopardy?" She frowned. "Those children are my life. All I do from morning to night is think about their health and well-being. And part of that scenario is having their father with them and not held hostage by a rogue freak." She withdrew her hand from his arm. "For your information, I've hired Somer permanently to be the babies' bodyguard. I doubt you'll be any more comfortable with that decision, but I hope that when you've had time to think about it, you'll appreciate the choice. Somer and Dr. Brody are marrying the week after Christmas, so she'll be living locally, and I can't think of anyone I'd rather have guarding my children. So you see, Galen, I do think about the children's safety."

He hesitated. "Isn't this something we should have discussed?"

"Not while you're convinced that the only way to deal with the problem is for our family to be separated. If we do that, Wolf wins." It broke Rose's heart just to imagine it. "You of all people should understand what it does to a family to be apart from the ones they love. And I know that if I leave, the separation will be permanent," she said slowly. "Your job is here, your place is in New Mexico. If I'm in Canada or Australia or Hawaii, wherever you decide to hide me, the children would grow up without a father. And that's what I'm really fighting for—my babies' right to grow up with you in their lives."

His mobile rang, interrupting what he was about to say. She waited for him to take the call, surprised when his face lit up. He asked a couple of questions, and she realized it was from someone at the hospital.

He clicked off his cell and stood. "Let's get the coffee and whatnot to go. That was the hospital."

Fear flew into her chest. She jumped to her feet, heart pounding. "Is Riley all right?"

"He's wonderful," Galen said. "The doctor says Riley can come home."

"Oh, Galen!" They hugged each other, and Rose thought this was the greatest moment of their marriage. Even though things had been hard lately between them, it felt as if they were close again. She closed her eyes, enjoying the feeling of Galen's arms around her, then realized tears were streaming down her face. He gently wiped them away. "It's the best news I could have gotten this Christmas," she told him. "Let's hurry!"

She grabbed their coffees and cake. Galen helped her into the truck and they headed to the hospital. Neither one said a thing about the angry words between them. Rose stared out the window, barely able to think about anything but Riley's homecoming.

Then she realized it wasn't time for Galen to be here. He was never back in Tempest this early. In the past week or so—ever since she'd shot Wolf—he'd mainly returned at night.

"Why are you in Tempest at four in the afternoon?" she asked.

"I wanted to check on you. Mack told me where I could find you."

"You could have called. I would have come home if I'd known you were back." She turned her eyes from the holiday-decorated shops to look at him.

"I could have, but I was hoping to do some shopping with you. I had promised you I would, and I wanted to keep that promise. So I took the afternoon off to spend with you. That was part of why I'm here."

She hadn't thought he wanted to spend time with her after she'd broken Running Bear's one cardinal rule: don't harm his son Wolf.

"But the real reason you came back is because you were hoping to talk some sense into me. Make me understand why you feel so strongly about me taking the children and going somewhere safer," she said, her heart sinking. "Not just because you wanted to keep a promise to me."

"It's a conversation best had another time, I think."

It was a conversation best ignored altogether. "Maybe another time we can shop," she murmured. "I've gotten just about everything I need for under the tree, and for the babies."

When Rose looked out the window again, even the wreaths on the lampposts failed to put any holiday spirit into her heart.

But her son was coming home—and that was Christmas enough.

GALEN DIDN'T KNOW what to say when his normally chatty wife went quiet. He would have expected her to be jumping for joy that Riley was coming home.

This had to get worked out soon. In a way, he hadn't ended up in any better a situation than his brothers, who he'd ribbed for putting the cart before the horse in the pursuit of their wives. They'd done baby first, then marriage. He'd done marriage first, then babies—then nothing.

Maybe his way hadn't been better. There was a good chance Rose finally agreed with Mack's warning against marrying into the Callahan clan. Perhaps she regretted the decision. Galen was so afraid that was true.

If he were in her cute little winter boots, he'd probably regret marrying him.

He pulled into the hospital parking lot as fat snowflakes began falling. "We may have a white Christmas."

"That would be pretty." Rose wrapped her scarf around her neck and got out, and he hurried around the truck to put his hand under her elbow so she wouldn't slip.

She pulled away, her smile a brief one. "I'm all right. Thank you."

"Rose—"

"Galen," Rose said, "I just want to get Riley now."

She definitely didn't want to talk about the status of their marriage. It was clear she had no intention of leaving Tempest.

By the set of Rose's face as she refused to look at him, he knew that conversation was a no-go. He decided it would be best to suck it up and leave that particular topic for another time.

They went to the neonatal nursery, and a nurse came to greet them. "You're here to take Riley Galen Chacon Callahan home? May I see identification, please? That guard over there insists everyone must have identification, as I'm sure you're aware, and hospital policy is the same."

"Yes," Rose and Galen said at the same time, reaching for their IDs. They glanced at each other, then to Riley's bassinet.

Galen smiled with pride at his son. "He's a big boy now, huh?"

"I think so," Rose said, smiling in turn as the nurse took Riley from his bassinet for a last diaper change. "He looks so strong!"

His son wasn't strong. He was the smallest, frailest of the bunch. Yet Galen felt hope spring inside him that his child was out of the woods, had time to grow big and tall.

He didn't want his boys to grow up like the Callahan cousins and his family had. Rose just had to understand that it was better to go away now rather than later. He glanced at the guard, who loomed in the corridor outside the nursery. Galen didn't recognize him. "I'm surprised hospital staff keeps a guard for the neonatal unit."

The nurse appeared surprised. "You assigned that guard, Mr. Callahan. He's here on your orders. In fact, he's rarely left his post."

Galen whipped around to look at the man again, but he was gone. Rose glanced at him in surprise, but he shook his head. "I just forgot, with all the hiring at the ranch."

The nurse brought Riley out, and Galen took the baby in his arms. "Look at you, son," he said proudly. "Daddy's Mighty Mouse."

"Let me have him. You check us out." Rose could hardly wait to get her hands on their child, Galen noted with pride. He smiled, loving how her face lit with joy, how her fingers eagerly touched their little baby's cheek.

"Come on, babe," Galen said a sudden huskiness in his voice. "Let's take our boy home."

He glanced back at the hallway, but the guard still hadn't returned. If a "Mr. Callahan" had assigned that guard, he'd be curious to know which one of his brothers had opted for that particular baby gift.

"Can you hang on a second, Rose?" Galen asked, pulling out his mobile to make a call.

She smiled and went to talk to some of the nurses about Riley, delighted to be taking her son home. Galen watched her, his heart huge with happiness and pride. She was the most beautiful woman he'd ever laid eyes on, and she'd given him the dreams of his heart.

Yet the mysterious guard bothered him.

"Jace," Galen said when his brother answered the phone. "There's a bodyguard that was assigned to Riley by a Mr. Callahan, supposedly. He's been out here every day. When we came to take Riley home, he disappeared into thin air. I know for a fact that no bodyguard on the Rancho Diablo payroll was assigned to Riley. Do you know anything about this?"

After a moment, Jace chuckled. "I bet I know who hired that bodyguard, Galen."

He blinked. "Who?"

"Think outside the box, way outside the box. See if you come up with the same idea I did."

Galen turned over possible options in his mind. "A Callahan, of course, because the nurse thought I'd hired him."

"It would have to be a Callahan. The hospital doesn't allow just anybody to stand in the hall and say he's guarding a baby. He has to have credentials, and approval from the administration. Aren't you supposed to be the brain in the family?"

"I am the brain in the family." Galen looked at Riley as he lay happily in his mother's arms, saying goodbye to all the nurses who'd taken such good care of him. "But if not you, then—"

"Didn't the nurse say it was a Mr. Callahan, bro, who had assigned the guard? How about Chacon Callahan. Our father, Carlos."

Galen's eyes went huge. "How can that be?"

"Ask the chief. He won't confirm our guess but you'll know by the stoic expression he always wears. But you and I are old enough to remember our father. You know the kind of man Dad was, and I don't doubt for a minute that protecting the next generation of our family would be second nature to him." Jace laughed again. "Just call it a Callahan Christmas miracle, and take your family home. Merry Christmas, big brother."

Shivers ran over Galen as he thought about Jace's words. Of course. It made perfect sense. Carlos wasn't going to leave any member of his family behind. They were a team; they were together forever.

In spirit and in heart.

And it was a miracle, a gift from the past that told him the future was going to be wonderfully blessed.

ONCE ROSE PUT Riley in his bassinet next to his brothers, it was as if the pieces of her heart suddenly fit together again, a puzzle completed.

"This is how it should be," she whispered. "This is Christmas."

Galen put his arm around her shoulder. The boys calmed, seemed content to be close together once more.

Rose's heart filled with more happiness than she'd ever known, and tears welled up in her eyes. "They're perfect," she said. "It's a miracle."

Galen's arm tightened on her, then he turned her toward him and kissed her gently. "It is a miracle. A Callahan Christmas miracle."

"I'd almost stopped believing," she said, staring into his eyes. "Christmas never really filled my heart. But now I feel it, Galen. And I know everything's going to be all right."

He hugged her to him, wrapping her against his strong chest. She could hear his heart beating, feel his arms tighten around her. "It's going to be all right. It's going to be better than all right," he said. "This is the first day. Everything from here on out is special, because we're all together."

She looked up at him, hope blossoming in her heart. "We can't let anything, or anyone, split up our family."

"I know. You're right. I shouldn't have doubted you. Next time, we'll work together on everything." He kissed her forehead, then her lips. "Now that Riley's home, I can see the future so much better."

Her face glowed with happiness. "Oh, Galen. You feel it, too. You know we belong together as a family."

He did know. He couldn't surrender to the fear. Ash had once told him he was making decisions from fear.

His sister was right. His wife was right.

He would never again make that mistake. The past few weeks of distance between him and Rose had been so hard on him. He belonged with his family. They made him strong, made him a better man. "I do know."

"Does that mean—"

"Yes. It means we'll all live here, or at Rancho Diablo, wherever you want to be. You, me, the babies. Mack, even, if he wants to be part of the clan."

"But together," Rose said. "No more trying to send me and the children off?"

Galen shook his head, looking down at his sons. What other decision could he make? He couldn't give this up for anything, and somehow, they'd make it work, even if he had to pay a platoon of bodyguards. "We stay together."

"I just know your parents would want us to make an effort to be a family. They gave up so much so you could have a chance at happiness." Rose laid her head on his chest, her heart practically soaring inside her. "Are you sure you'll be okay with this?"

"Carlos and Julia do want us to be together, and I know that now. It's not going to be easy," Galen said. "You know Wolf's going to make our lives miserable."

"He won't make mine miserable," Rose said. "I'm raising three Callahans. He'd better watch out for my team."

Galen closed his eyes and smiled. There was nothing he could do. It was just as Running Bear had said: he'd married a warrior. She wasn't going to retreat, and she'd fight whoever tried to stand in her way.

"You know," Galen said, "some people might think you're stubborn, babe."

She smiled against his chest. "Some people might, and they'd be right."

The two of them looked down at their children. "Triplets. You gave me triplets," Galen said, unable to help the wonder in his voice. "Three special little boys."

"Yes, I did," Rose said. "And I have something else you might like for Christmas, as well."

"Oh?" He studied his darling wife, noting the sudden mischievous glint in her eyes. "What would that be?"

"I had my doctor's appointment. And she told me..." Rose began. Then she whispered something in his ear, so that his sons couldn't hear their mother proposing something of a delightfully naughty nature, a Christmas surprise, to their father.

Galen scooped her up in his arms and carried her to their room. "Good things come to those who wait," he told his beautiful wife. "And then again, good things come faster to those who don't want to wait another moment."

Rose laughed. "Merry Christmas, husband."

"Merry Christmas, wife."

And they proceeded to enjoy Christmas as fast as they possibly could. As far as Galen was concerned, this was the best Christmas ever. It was magic. It was complete happiness—it was everything he'd been dreaming of before he'd even known that the dream existed in his heart.

Miraculous.

Epilogue

The thing about the magic wedding dress, as far as Rose could see, was that it was just so sumptuously beautiful. Of course, she didn't give too much credence to all the fairy tales and legends surrounding it, but as she studied the dress in the bag—finally her turn in Fiona's attic— she saw the moment she'd long waited for.

Her chance to be a true Callahan bride.

The guests were waiting downstairs, as was her husband, this lovely Christmas Eve. They'd opted to have a quick vow renewal before candlelight services, a romantic icing on the holiday cake. Rose could hardly wait.

"You're lovely," she whispered to the gown. "I've waited a long time to try you on. Fiona promises that you'll be a perfect fit, which will indeed be a magical moment."

Of course, she would have married Galen again if she'd had to wear a potato sack. After all the turmoil in the first few weeks of their marriage, she was more than ready to start over with vows of love, and their babies present.

She slipped the dress from the bag, then stepped into it, holding her breath as she moved closer to the cheval mirror. In the lamplight she could see twinkles and sparkles on the splendid fabric, and as she pulled the dress up to her shoulders, it wrapped around her with a whisper of perfection.

She smiled as she looked at the dress in the mirror. "You're everything I ever heard, or ever imagined," she told it. "Thank you for being the most beautiful dress I've ever seen."

More sparkles seemed to glimmer, cascading around her. Rose did a little turn to see the back—and realized Galen was standing next to her, his eyes smiling with love and happiness.

"I love you," she told her husband. "I've loved you from afar for so long, since the first time I ever tried to bid on you at the Christmas ball. I love the fact that we'll always be together now. You and me, and the babies. Our wonderful family."

He nodded, and she could see in his eyes that he completely agreed with her, that whatever happened in the future, they would always face it together.

And then he disappeared.

Rose shivered. It had been so real! Galen had been standing next to her—she hadn't imagined gazing into his eyes. The moment had been for the two of them alone.

And yet he wasn't here now. The attic door had never opened.

Rose turned back to the mirror, and smiled at the dress.

"Thank you," she said. "Thank you so very much for showing me the man of my dreams. I'm the luckiest woman in the world."

All her dreams had come positively, blissfully true.

CHRISTMAS MORNING, the moment Rose had long been waiting for, bloomed bright and sunny over the house in Tempest. Icicles dripped as they melted, and the sun beamed on the white snow.

She had her three sons and her husband—and it was a beautiful, amazing day.

"Merry Christmas!" she said, waking Galen with a kiss.

"Merry Christmas, wife." He snuggled her against him, holding her as close as he could. "The babies are so quiet. I think they were worn out from the wedding. They got passed around by half of Diablo."

"It was the most beautiful wedding ever." Rose smiled at him. "That was a pretty romantic idea you had, husband."

He grinned, pleased. "It was, wasn't it?"

She straddled him with a wicked smile. "So tell me, what's this rumor that Callahans are hard to get to an altar—and yet somehow, most or all of you seem to do it twice?"

"Yeah, we haven't quite figured that out yet." He pulled her down to him for a kiss. "But it's working for us."

"That's true." Rose kissed her husband, then rolled out of bed. "Your Christmas surprise comes later. I'm dying to see the babies. And give you your present."

"I had a present in mind," he said, getting out of bed, "but it involved unwrapping you, not a box."

She giggled. "I've got Mack and Somer babysitting all afternoon. You're getting a mini-honeymoon today, don't worry."

"That's better." A pleased smile lit Galen's face. "I like this sexy side of you, Mrs. Callahan."

She loved knowing that. She dragged him out of the room by the hand to find the babies.

"Look at them," he said.

The three little boys lay next to each other in the jammies that Fiona's friends had made them, like tiny Christmas elves. "I never thought I'd be so happy," Rose said.

He put an arm around her. "I never thought I'd have three sons. You never fail to amaze me, beautiful."

She smiled. "I believe you provided the necessary ingredient."

He grinned hugely. "Love?"

"Exactly." She winked.

"I do love you so much," Galen said, and she could hear his heart in his words.

"I love you, too."

They stood watching their babies for a few more moments, enjoying their first Christmas together. The tree twinkled and the fire crackled, and it felt so wonderful to be a family that Rose couldn't imagine anything better in her life.

"I have a gift for you." Galen went to the tree, pulled out a tiny red box with a big gold ribbon on it. "Merry Christmas, sweetheart."

She smiled, shook the box. "Hmm. No sound. Must be air."

He sat on the couch and pulled her into his lap. "Must be. Open it and see."

Rose undid the bow and unwrapped the paper, to find a velvety jeweler's box. She looked at Galen.

"Well, I figured you deserved something very small for giving me three fine sons," Galen said, kissing her. "Let's see if it fits."

She opened the box, and smiled at the engagement ring with three oval diamonds on it. "It's beautiful, Galen. Thank you." He slipped the ring on her finger, and, of course, it fit perfectly.

"I never had a chance to get you what I really wanted to. We settled for bands the first time around. So I wanted to make sure you knew how much I truly love you."

She kissed him deeply, melting against him. "I love you, too."

It felt wonderful to be in his arms, together forever.

"But you know," Rose said, hopping out of his lap, "we need to get dressed. I have a family photographer arriving soon."

"On Christmas Day?"

"Yes." She nodded definitively. "You'll need blue jeans, white shirt, hat optional. I want it to be comfy, a family portrait of our first Christmas together. I hope you don't mind."

"That's a great idea. How did you think of it?"

Rose smiled, unable to keep the teasing note from her voice. "Well, it all came about when you talked me into going into the cave."

"Here we go," Galen said.

She laughed. "No, really. And while I was down there, I saw that portrait of Running Bear. Remember?"

"I know you mentioned it. I was out cold when I was taken there, so I never saw it."

"I know," Rose said. "And that's too bad. But I started thinking about how important it is for family to be commemorated, and how much it means to remember the important moments. So I decided I wanted our first

Christmas together to be captured. We'll put it in your office at Rancho Diablo."

Galen grinned. "Thank you. Come here and let me thank you properly."

"Actually, I'm not quite done with your present," Rose said. "The family portrait we're having taken is a companion piece to something else I want to hang in your office." She pulled a big, brown-wrapped package from behind the tree and handed it to him. "This is your real gift, Galen. Merry Christmas."

"Those are my real gifts, over there," he said, pointing to his sons. "Rudolph, Donner and Blitzen, according to the names on their outfits."

She laughed. "Open your gift."

He unwrapped the brown paper, and held up a newly framed portrait of Running Bear. "This is amazing," Galen said, staring at the likeness. "The artist did a fabulous job capturing Grandfather. How did you ever…" He turned to look at her, his eyes wide. "Oh, no. You didn't get this out of the cave."

Rose smiled and got in his lap for a fast kiss he was too stunned to return.

"Tell me you didn't go back to the cave to get this out. Rose, promise me you'll never go back there again."

She got the giggles just looking at the astonishment on her husband's face. "I will never go back there again, unless you decide you need me to help you on another Callahan escapade."

He put the portrait down, held her close to him. "You're going to drive me mad, aren't you?"

"I plan to keep our marriage exciting."

He shook his head. "You didn't—"

"I didn't. I promise." She kissed Galen. "I told Running Bear I'd seen his portrait in the cave, and it dawned on me that I hadn't seen any pictures of him around Rancho Diablo. And since he's the heart and soul of the ranch, I want our sons to know him, and be able to remember him always. So I asked him to sit for a portrait for your Christmas present." She shrugged. "One day I came into the house, and this was in front of the tree with my name on it."

Rose looked at Galen, then said, "It's the one from the cave. I recognize it. Of course, I didn't ask him where he'd gotten it, but I knew. I just thanked him, and told him this was exactly what I wanted to give you for Christmas."

Galen shook his head. "My grandfather is definitely a spirit of his own understanding."

"Yes."

"I think I'll put it in the boys' nursery, along with this," he said, getting down the Christmas stocking with her name on it. "There's something in here I want you to have."

She pulled out the little silver statue of a Diablo mustang she'd taken from the cave so long ago. "Thank you, Galen."

"Thank *you*," he said. "If it hadn't been for your bravery, none of this would have ever come into my life. Not the babies, not you, nothing."

She kissed him, and they held each other for a long time, there in front of the fire, until the babies began moving, ready to share Christmas Day with their parents.

It was the most wonderful day of their married life, and Rose wanted to remember it forever.

And that's the way the family portrait looked, two

months later, in its place over the mantel in the house in Diablo: Galen, Rose, little Mack, Ross and Riley in front of the Christmas tree, with Running Bear's portrait leaning against the lovely wrapped presents, and the silver filigree Diablo mustang placed on a tree branch. It was all there in the picture that was taken that day, alive for posterity—and every time Rose looked at the wonderful portrait, she smiled at the miracle of Christmas framed forever.

It *was* a Callahan Christmas miracle, and Rose and Galen celebrated that miracle each and every day of their lives.

Together.

* * * * *

Jace is the last Callahan bachelor up for grabs.
Find out who tames him in
HER CALLAHAN FAMILY MAN,
coming January 2014
only from Harlequin American Romance!

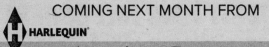
#1477 THE TEXAS CHRISTMAS GIFT
McCabe Homecoming • by Cathy Gillen Thacker

Eve Loughlin is completely unsentimental about Christmas.
That is, until she falls for Derek McCabe and his infant daughter,
Tiffany, who have Christmas in their hearts all year long!

#1478 THE COWBOY'S CHRISTMAS SURPRISE
Forever, Texas • by Marie Ferrarella

Cowboy Ray Rodriguez has been looking for love in all the
wrong places. He never suspected after one night with a
longtime friend, the sweet and loyal Holly, he'd be tempted
with forever.

#1479 SECOND CHANCE CHRISTMAS
The Colorado Cades • by Tanya Michaels

Bad boy Justin Cade has no interest in starting a family. Yet,
thanks to Elisabeth Donnelly, his ex, and the six-year-old
girl she's adopted, Justin finds himself visiting Santa Claus,
decorating Christmas trees...and falling in love.

#1480 THE SEAL'S CHRISTMAS TWINS
Operation: Family • by Laura Marie Altom

Navy SEAL Mason Brown gets the shock of his life when his
ex-wife leaves him custody of her twin daughters in her will.
He's a soldier—not daddy material!

REQUEST YOUR FREE BOOKS!
2 FREE NOVELS PLUS 2 FREE GIFTS!

HARLEQUIN

American ★ Romance®

LOVE, HOME & HAPPINESS

YES! Please send me 2 FREE Harlequin® American Romance® novels and my 2 FREE gifts (gifts are worth about $10). After receiving them, if I don't wish to receive any more books, I can return the shipping statement marked "cancel." If I don't cancel, I will receive 4 brand-new novels every month and be billed just $4.74 per book in the U.S. or $5.24 per book in Canada. That's a savings of at least 14% off the cover price! It's quite a bargain! Shipping and handling is just 50¢ per book in the U.S. and 75¢ per book in Canada.* I understand that accepting the 2 free books and gifts places me under no obligation to buy anything. I can always return a shipment and cancel at any time. Even if I never buy another book, the two free books and gifts are mine to keep forever.

154/354 HDN F4YN

Name	(PLEASE PRINT)	
Address		Apt. #
City	State/Prov.	Zip/Postal Code

Signature (if under 18, a parent or guardian must sign)

Mail to the Harlequin® Reader Service:
IN U.S.A.: P.O. Box 1867, Buffalo, NY 14240-1867
IN CANADA: P.O. Box 609, Fort Erie, Ontario L2A 5X3

**Want to try two free books from another line?
Call 1-800-873-8635 or visit www.ReaderService.com.**

* Terms and prices subject to change without notice. Prices do not include applicable taxes. Sales tax applicable in N.Y. Canadian residents will be charged applicable taxes. Offer not valid in Quebec. This offer is limited to one order per household. Not valid for current subscribers to Harlequin American Romance books. All orders subject to credit approval. Credit or debit balances in a customer's account(s) may be offset by any other outstanding balance owed by or to the customer. Please allow 4 to 6 weeks for delivery. Offer available while quantities last.

Your Privacy—The Harlequin® Reader Service is committed to protecting your privacy. Our Privacy Policy is available online at www.ReaderService.com or upon request from the Harlequin Reader Service.

We make a portion of our mailing list available to reputable third parties that offer products we believe may interest you. If you prefer that we not exchange your name with third parties, or if you wish to clarify or modify your communication preferences, please visit us at www.ReaderService.com/consumerschoice or write to us at Harlequin Reader Service Preference Service, P.O. Box 9062, Buffalo, NY 14269. Include your complete name and address.

HAR13R

SPECIAL EXCERPT FROM

 HARLEQUIN®

American Romance®

Read on for a sneak peek of
THE TEXAS CHRISTMAS GIFT
by Cathy Gillen Thacker

Eve Laughlin is completely unsentimental about
Christmas…until she meets the very attractive
Derek McCabe

This was what Eve wanted, too. Even if she would have preferred not to admit it. Before she could stop herself, before she could think of all the reasons why not, she let Derek pull her closer still. His head dipped. Her breath caught, and her eyes closed. And then all was lost in the first luscious feeling of his lips lightly pressed against hers.

It was a cautious kiss. A gentle kiss that didn't stay gallant for long. At her first quiver of sensation, he flattened his hands over her spine and deepened the kiss, seducing her with the heat of his mouth and the sheer masculinity of his tall, strong body. Yearning swept through her in great enervating waves. Unable to help herself, Eve went up on tiptoe, leaning into his embrace. Throwing caution to the wind, she wreathed her arms about his neck and kissed him back. Not tentatively, not sweetly, but with all the hunger and need she felt. And to her wonder and delight, he kissed her back in kind, again and again and again.

Derek had only meant to show Eve they had chemistry. Amazing chemistry that would convince her to go out with him, at least once. He hadn't expected to feel tenderness well inside him, even as his body went hard with desire. He hadn't expected to want to make love to her here and now, in this empty house. But sensing that total surrender would be a mistake, he tamped down his own desire and let the kiss come to a slow, gradual end.

Eve stepped backward, too, a mixture of surprise and pleasure on her face. Her breasts were rising and falling quickly, and her lips were moist. Amazement at the potency of their attraction, and something else a lot more cautious, appeared in her eyes. Eve drew a breath, and then anger flashed. "That was a mistake."

Derek understood her need to play down what had just happened, even as he saw no reason to pretend they hadn't enjoyed themselves immensely. "Not in my book," he murmured, still feeling a little off balance himself. In fact, he was ready for a whole lot more.

Can Derek convince Eve to take a chance
on him this Christmas?

Find out in
THE TEXAS CHRISTMAS GIFT
by Cathy Gillen Thacker
Available December 3, only from
Harlequin® American Romance®.

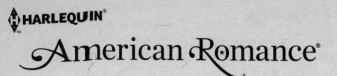

HARLEQUIN®
American Romance®

Since the first grade, Holly Johnson has known that
Ramon Rodriguez is the only man for her. But the carefree,
determinedly single Texas cowboy with the killer smile
doesn't have a clue. Until they share a dance and a kiss…
and Ray finally sees his best friend for the woman in love
she is. Now that he realizes what he's been missing,
Ray plans to make up for lost time…starting with the
three little words Holly's waited thirteen years to hear.

The Cowboy's Christmas Surprise
by *USA TODAY* bestselling author
MARIE FERRARELLA

Available November 5,
from Harlequin® American Romance®.

www.Harlequin.com

HAR75482

HARLEQUIN®

American Romance®

A Christmas to Remember

Ski-lodge manager Elisabeth is the responsible
Donnelly twin. It wasn't like her to fall in love with
ski patroller Justin Cade, but it was *just* like him to
dump her when things got serious.

Now he's suddenly back in her life, and the timing
couldn't be worse. Elisabeth has plans to marry a
successful businessman and Christmas is right around
the corner. Falling for Justin again would not be the
sensible thing to do. But maybe, for once in her life,
Elisabeth should follow her heart instead of her head.

Second Chance Christmas

by TANYA MICHAELS

Available November 5,
from Harlequin® American Romance®.

www.Harlequin.com

HAR75483